M

Tapply, William G
The snake eater

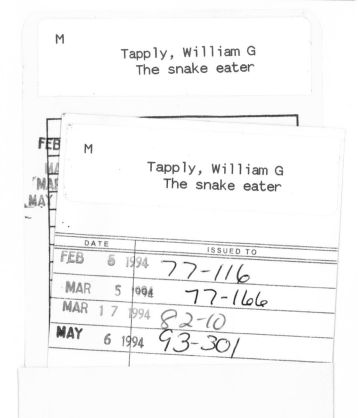

M

Tapply, William G
The snake eater

DATE	ISSUED TO
FEB 5 1994	77-116
MAR 5 1994	77-166
MAR 17 1994	82-10
MAY 6 1994	93-301

THE SNAKE EATER

Also by William G. Tapply

THE SNAKE EATER

WILLIAM G. TAPPLY

OTTO PENZLER BOOKS

NEW YORK

Otto Penzler Books
129 W. 56th Street
New York, NY 10019
(Editorial Offices only)

Macmillan Publishing Company
866 Third Avenue
New York, NY 10022

Maxwell Macmillan Canada, Inc.
1200 Eglinton Avenue East
Suite 200
Don Mills, Ontario M3C 3N1

Macmillan Publishing Company is part of the Maxwell Communication Group of Companies.

Library of Congress Cataloging-in-Publication Data

Tapply, William G.
    The snake eater / by William G. Tapply.
        p.   cm.
    ISBN 1-883402-04-2
    1. Coyne, Brady (Fictitious character)—Fiction.   2. Lawyers—Massachusetts—Boston—Fiction.   3. Boston (Mass.)—Fiction.
I. Title.
PS3570.A568S65   1993
813'.54—dc20   93-19362

Otto Penzler Books are available at special discounts for bulk purchases for sales promotions, premiums, fund-raising, or educational use. For details, contact:

Special Sales Director
Macmillan Publishing Company
866 Third Avenue
New York, NY 10022

Printed in the United States of America

For Michael

ACKNOWLEDGMENTS

A writer feeds off the love and understanding of family and friends during the long self-absorbed process of novel-making. He is generally not good company. My kids, for some reason, seem to love me no matter how weird I get. My writing group keeps reminding me that it's supposed to be hard. Andy Gill, Elliot Schildkrout, Steve Cooper, Randy Paulsen, and Jon Kolb just pour me a Daniel's, deal another hand, tell trout stories, and, in a pinch, analyze my dreams.

For their indispensable help with this manuscript, I also want to thank Jane Rabe, Rick Boyer, Betsy Rapoport, Alcinda VanDeurson, Jed Mattes, and Michele Slung.

THE SNAKE EATER

PROLOGUE

He should've taken a taxi.

That was his first thought after he completed his descent and began to shoulder through the bodies toward the front of the platform.

He held his briefcase flat against his crotch, like a shield. Women aren't the only ones who have to watch out for subway gropers. He'd learned that from personal experience.

As he wedged his way forward, the bodies closed in around him. Old, young, black, white, male, female. Not people. Just bodies. And as the bodies closed in, so did their heat. And their odors, all mingled, the stench of a hundred human bodies, smells of sex and anxiety and fear, farts and urine and sweat and booze and garlic all mixed in a disgusting stew of human stink.

He tried breathing through his mouth. The odors became tastes. He was afraid he might gag.

He tugged at the knot in his necktie, felt dribbles of

sweat begin to trickle down his sides, dampen the insides of his thighs, soak the back of his shirt under his linen jacket.

He pulled the briefcase tighter against him, grateful for the thin but comforting barrier.

The crush of bodies around him forced him up against a man who stood solid and unmovable in front of him. He was a head taller, this man, with a brown neck as thick as a telephone pole and a shaved brown scalp that glistened in the piss-colored light. Another body nudged him from behind, then settled against him. More bodies, bodies on both sides, bodies everywhere. They pressed his arms against his sides, holding him immobile with the heavy briefcase tight against his middle.

It was oddly silent there beneath the street. Some muffled human sounds. Breathing, grunting. No distinguishable voices. Distant mechanical sounds. Somewhere on the platform a radio. Rock music and static.

Why in hell hadn't he taken a taxi?

He felt the vibrations through the soles of his feet. As the tremoring grew, the crowd seemed to shake itself like a dog in a dream, muttering, twitching its separate parts to separate rhythms as it came awake, and then he heard the rumble, and it became a roar, and with it the metal-on-metal screech as the train approached the platform.

Thank God.

The bodies pressed tighter against him, forcing his face up against the damp shirt of the enormous man in front of him.

A hand snaked around from behind him, then an arm half encircled him. A forearm against his chest forced the top half of his body backward. And an odd pinprick low on his back, and then—

Oh, Jesus! A shaft of pain, sudden, searing, unbearable. He threw back his head, he opened his mouth, he knew he screamed. He heard nothing but the metallic squeal of brakes and the hiss and rumble of the engine. He screamed again and again as a red-hot arrow of indescribable pain burned toward his heart and bodies surged around him and the train roared and screeched.

That arm around his chest held him impaled on his pain. His knees buckled. His legs were suddenly cold, numb. He became detached from his body. He felt himself float above the crowd and drift there, separate now from the mob, looking down at them, looking down at himself and his pain.

But he saw only fog.

He had the urge to laugh. He instantly forgot why.

A gentle voice in his ear said, "Thank you. I'll take that." The briefcase. It was gone. His shield. Now his groin—

Another pain, quick and hard, rammed into the core of his soul, and with that ramrod of pain came the understanding of what that kind of pain meant.

The sudden urge to vomit. No strength for it. And then he felt himself spinning, spiraling.

The bottom half of his body began to melt. A snowman on a hot sidewalk. So that's how it felt to be dying.

To be dying.

Christ. Oh good Jesus Christ forever and ever world without end amen.

The book. The damn book.

It's true.

If he could just remain upright he wouldn't die. Nobody died standing up. That's true, isn't it? He tried to lift his hands, to grab the shoulder of the big man in front of him, something to hang on to, to keep him upright, to keep him alive. But his fingers were numb and his arms refused to move. He felt himself tilt sideways, settle momentarily against the man's broad, wet back, slip, slide, collapse.

Where are you, honey? Sweetheart? Are you there?

They were stepping around him, avoiding him. From somewhere far away he heard a woman's voice. "See? The bums are wearing neckties these days. Banker, lawyer, ha? High roller from Wall Street, ha? See? That's what's happening to them."

His mind formed the words "Help me." He thought he spoke those words. He couldn't hear his own voice. Couldn't hear anything. Just a hum, growing fainter.

Should've taken a taxi. . . .

1

It was the summer's first heat wave, and I was putting my pinstripe away for the weekend when Charlie McDevitt called.

"Coyne," I said. I wedged the phone against my shoulder and sat on the edge of my bed to tug at my pantlegs.

"Hey," he said.

"What's up?"

"Friend of mine needs a lawyer."

"I litigate, therefore I am," I said. "My motto."

"Ha," he said. "I know you. You take on new clients the way Red Auerbach signs rejects off the waiver wire."

"Rarely," I said. "You're right."

"Anyway, this one's criminal, not civil. But he needs you."

"Tell me." I dropped my pants in a heap on the floor. I lay back on my bed and lit a cigarette.

Charlie cleared his throat. "Guy name of Daniel

McCloud got picked up this afternoon in Wilson Falls, charged with possession, possession with intent, and trafficking."

"Where in hell is Wilson Falls?"

"Little nothing town out in the Connecticut Valley. More or less across the river from Northampton."

"They holding him?"

"Yes. Arraignment won't be till Monday."

"Was he?"

"What, trafficking?"

"Yes. Was he trafficking?"

"He grew marijuana in his backyard. The cops came with a warrant, ripped up his garden, filled several trash bags. Not to mention all the incriminating odds and ends they found in the house."

"Trafficking includes cultivation," I said. "Fifty pounds means trafficking. That's a felony worth two-and-a-half to fifteen. Must've been a major-league garden. What about priors?"

"One year suspended in '79 for possession. He also admitted to sufficient facts in '76. That's supposed to be sealed, of course, but . . ."

"But," I said, "the court sees it on his record anyway. Which makes this his third time up." I paused to stub out my cigarette, then said, "Sorry, pal. No deal. Friend or no friend, I'm not defending some drug dealer. I don't need that kind of business."

"He's no dealer, Brady. He grows it for himself. He's sick. It helps him. It's the only thing that helps him."

"Sure."

"Really," said Charlie. "Daniel doesn't deal. He needs you. This is a favor for me."

"He needs a good criminal lawyer, all right," I said. "So why me?"

"You'll like Daniel. And you're good."

"Christ, you know how much criminal work I've done lately?"

"I know what you *can* do, Brady. All those wills and divorces must drive you batshit after a while."

"That they do. So what's this Daniel McCloud to you?"

"He's just this quiet guy from Georgia who tried to get some money out of Uncle Sam, which is how I met him. He spent six years in the jungles of Indochina, got himself Agent Oranged, and not a penny for his misery. He runs a little bait-and-tackle shop on the banks of the Connecticut, likes to fish and hunt and hang out in the woods. Prison would kill him. Literally."

"And they nailed him growing fifty pounds of marijuana?"

"Looks that way."

"I don't know what the hell you expect me to do."

"You can start by getting him out on bail."

"Wilson Falls," I said, "is a long drive from Boston."

"So you'd better get an early start," said Charlie.

"Um," I said. "Tell me something."

"What's that?"

"This is one of your *pro bono* deals, right?"

"Nope."

"He can afford me?"

"I think so, yes."

"Be damned," I muttered.

A cop brought Daniel McCloud into the little conference room in the Wilson Falls police station on Saturday morning. He sat down at the scarred wooden table and looked at me without curiosity, gratitude, anger, or fear. Without, in fact, any expression whatsoever. Except, maybe, patience.

I held my hand to him. "Brady Coyne. I'm a lawyer."

He took my hand briefly. His handshake was neither robust nor enthusiastic, but I sensed great strength in it. He said nothing.

"Charlie McDevitt asked me to come," I said.

"Charlie." He nodded. "A good man."

"He didn't call me until about seven last night. This was the earliest I could make it."

He shrugged.

"I hope you weren't worried?"

"Worried?"

"You know . . ."

"I was waiting." He said it as if waiting and worrying were not activities that could be conducted simultaneously.

"Did you sleep okay?"

"Nay. I didn't sleep at all. I hardly ever do."

"I won't be able to get you out of here until Monday," I said. "They don't do arraignments on weekends."

"I know that," said Daniel. "That's why they waited until Friday afternoon to come for me. It's that farkin' Oakley."

"Oakley?"

"The cop who arrested me."

"What about him?"

Daniel jerked one shoulder in a shrug. "He didn't have to wait until Friday afternoon. You see?"

He spoke softly, and I thought I detected just the hint of a Scottish burr mingling into his southern drawl. His voice was almost musical.

I shrugged. "I'm not sure."

"He doesn't like me."

"Why not?"

He shook his head. "I don't know. Maybe it's that my woman is black. See, Mr. Coyne, Wilson Falls is a small town. Everybody knows everybody else. Who they live with. What they grow in their garden. How much they'd enjoy a weekend in jail. He could've arrested me anytime."

"Well, regardless of all that," I said, "the first thing we've got to do is get you out of here. Can you get your hands on some cash?"

"I have some resources." He smiled. He had, I noticed, terrible teeth. They were gray and stubbed and gapped. Several were missing. Later he would tell me, "You sometimes forget to floss regularly in the jungle."

"I'll try to get you out on personal recognizance," I told him. "I doubt if it will work. They'll want to go high. The courts are making examples of their drug cases these days. I'll need to know some things."

"I could use a smoke," Daniel said suddenly.

"Oh, I'm sorry." I put my pack of Winstons onto the table. "Help yourself."

He glanced down at the cigarettes, then looked up at me and shrugged.

"Oh, Christ," I said. "You can't smoke that stuff here."

"It's my medicine," he said, and that's when I first noticed that beneath the table that separated us his right leg was jiggling furiously. I looked hard into his face and saw a tiny muscle twitching and jumping at the corner of his eye. Behind his mask of calm, Daniel McCloud was, I realized, in agony.

"Charlie told me you encountered Agent Orange over there."

"Aye."

"That's how you met him?"

"Yes. We thought our government would want to take care of us."

"And it didn't work out."

"We got nowhere. Charlie tried to help. Good fella, Charlie."

"We?"

He shrugged. "Sweeney and I. Sweeney's one of my buddies. We were S.F. together, got burned together, and —"

"S.F.?" I blurted.

He smiled. "S.F. Special Forces."

"You were a Green Beret?"

He rolled his eyes. "We *wore* the farkin' hats. A green beret is a hat, and it's a book and a movie and a song. But it's not a man. We didn't even like 'em. Nobody put 'em on except when they had to. Anyway, Sweeney and I tried to get some medical help from the government. But we didn't have cancer, we weren't dead, or even, as far as they would admit, dying. We couldn't prove what we got was from the Orange. So we had no case."

"And marijuana helps you."

"Aye. It helps the itching and the pain. It's the only thing that helps."

"How do you feel now?"

"Right this minute?"

"Yes."

He exhaled deeply. "It's driving me crazy, Mr. Coyne."

"How much do you smoke?"

"I need six to eight sticks a day."

"My God!"

He shrugged. Daniel shrugged often, I was beginning to notice. It seemed to be his primary form of expression. When he shrugged, he gave his shoulders a tiny twitch and darted his eyes upward. It wasn't a very dramatic shrug. "It's the only thing that'll help," he said.

"What about the trafficking charge?" I said. "Do you sell it?"

He leaned across the table and gave me a hard look. "I smoke it. What do you think I am?"

"A drug dealer, of course."

"Never," he said quietly.

I shrugged. "Charlie told me you had money."

"Aye. I have some. That's not where I got it."

"If I'm going to represent you, I've got to know."

He peered at me, then nodded. "I don't sell it, Mr. Coyne."

"Do you share it? The grass?"

"Aye. With Sweeney. He needs it, too, same as me.

And sometimes Cammie. She's my woman. Just a stick now and then. She keeps me company with it."

Daniel McCloud did not fit my mental image of a Green Beret. He stood no more than five-eight, and he looked overweight in his baggy chino pants. His sandy hair was thin and uncombed, his face pockmarked, and his eyes were a washed-out blue. He wore steel-rimmed glasses. I guessed he was in his late forties, although he looked ten years older than that.

He looked like a lot of other country boys I have known who get old early in life.

He also looked like a man with a terrible disease who had spent a sleepless night in jail without his medicine.

"At the arraignment Monday," I said, "I'll have to argue for reasonable bail. I need to know some things."

He nodded.

"How long have you lived in Wilson Falls?"

"Almost twenty years."

"Own your own home?"

"Aye."

"And a business?"

"I've got a shop. I sell bait and tackle, bow-hunting stuff."

"You're a fisherman?"

He smiled. "Aye. I grew up in the outdoors."

"I love fishing myself. Fly-fishing, mostly. Fly-fishing for trout."

"I look at it a little different," he said. "I go after whatever is there, and I catch 'em any way I can. I like to improvise. Same way I hunt. Bow 'n' arrows, snares, slingshots.

It's how I was brought up." He closed his eyes for a moment. When he opened them, I saw in them for the first time a hint of feeling, something other than the pain, although I couldn't identify that feeling. Wistfulness, maybe. Or loneliness. "My daddy was a poacher down in Monroe, Georgia," he said softly. "He taught me the woods. He killed deer with bows and arrows and spears he made himself, so the wardens wouldn't hear him. They all knew he did it. But he never once got caught. That was the fun he got out of it. That was his sport. Outwitting the wardens. Fishing and hunting weren't sports for him. He was a Scotsman. Knew the value of things. My daddy took game and fish when he needed it to feed us. Never more, never less. He taught me how to survive in the woods. I knew all about survival before I ever got to Fort Bragg. How to eat whatever you could find, how to disguise your smell, how to be invisible, how to distinguish all the different sounds in the woods, what it means when there are no sounds. My daddy made me eat bugs when I was six. After bugs, any kind of meat's pretty good. Better when you can cook it, but good anytime." Daniel shrugged. "He used to tell me, 'Son,' he'd say, 'they make the farkin' law because they need general guidelines. They try to hit an average with it. But that don't mean it's right for a particular person. Maybe a deer a year per man is a good guideline. But it ain't right for us. You've got to figger what's right for you. That's your law.'"

He looked at me and smiled. He was, after his fashion, giving me his defense. I guessed this was a long speech for Daniel McCloud.

"Like growing your own marijuana," I said. "That's your law."

He shook his head. "God's law. Not mine. My daddy told me that if it don't hurt anybody else, and it helps you, then it's God's law you should do it. He never broke God's law. Shit, neither did I. I guess we both broke man's law some. Difference is, my daddy never got caught."

We talked a while longer. Daniel told me what I needed to know to handle his arraignment on Monday. I tried to explain how it would go. "We'll wait around for a long time. Eventually it'll be your turn. They'll read the charges against you. We'll argue about your bail. The judge will set it, and if you can make it you'll be released. Then you and I can start thinking about the probable-cause hearing."

I told him they'd bring him to the district court in Northampton on Monday morning and I'd meet him there. I told him it was a lousy deal that he had to spend the weekend in jail, that if he'd been arrested any day but Friday or Saturday he'd be arraigned and out on bail the next day. He repeated that he knew "that farkin' Oakley" had come for him on Friday afternoon on purpose, because he had it in for him and wanted him to suffer. I asked him if he was suffering. He nodded and said yes, as a matter of fact, he was suffering terribly, and he said it in such a way to make me understand that he was familiar with suffering and tried not to let it bother him. I asked him if I could bring him something. The only thing that would help, he said, would be a few sticks of cannabis.

I told him I didn't think I'd be able to do that for him.

When we stood up and shook hands, Daniel said, "Can you get me out of here?"

I hesitated. Bail would come high. But I nodded and said, "Sure."

The smile he gave me showed me what I hadn't seen before—that Daniel McCloud, survivor of the terrors of the Southeast Asia jungles, was scared.

2

I arrived at the Northampton District Court on Monday morning for the nine o'clock criminal session. I sat on one of the benches among the lawyers, witnesses, and accused citizens, feeling tired and headachy from getting up early and driving the two hours from Boston to Northampton—a long straight monotonous shot out the Mass Pike to Springfield, then a quick jog north on 91.

I wished I'd had the foresight to sneak a cup of coffee into the courtroom with me.

At the table in front of the bench the clerk shuffled a large stack of manila folders. A pair of probation officers whispered at their table.

About ten after nine a uniformed officer led six or eight bleary-eyed men into the prisoners' dock. Daniel was the last of them. He looked out of place among the others, young men all, the weekend collection of lockups. Sobriety test and Breathalyzer flunkees, I guessed.

I jerked my chin at Daniel. He nodded to me.

His leg, I observed, was jiggling madly.

Then a side door opened and the judge came in. One of the officers said, "All rise."

We all rose.

A voice from the back of the courtroom mumbled, "Hear ye, hear ye," told us the Honorable Anthony Ropek was presiding, and concluded, "God save the Commonwealth of Massachusetts."

The judge sat. The officer said, "Be seated." The rest of us sat. The clerk leaned against the bench and conferred with the judge for at least five minutes. High drama.

Then the clerk returned to his table and began reciting names. To each one, the probation officers responded. Usually one of them would say, "Terminate and discharge." A couple of times they said, "Request default warrant." They directed their words to the judge. The clerk, however, ran the show.

It was all routine court business, and it gave me a chance to size up Judge Anthony Ropek. He was small and gray and businesslike as, with an unintelligible word and small gesture, he repeatedly gave his official endorsements to the requests of the probation officers. He was an old-timer, I guessed, still in district court after all these years, which meant that he'd probably been passed over for superior court or federal seats enough times to know that he wasn't going anywhere else. This I took to be a positive omen for Daniel. Judge Ropek didn't strike me as a man with a motive to build a reputation at the expense of an ailing Vietnam vet who grew his own marijuana.

After the probation cases came the weekend motor

vehicle cases. All involved drunk driving. Most of them pleaded guilty, were fined, had their licenses revoked, and were enrolled in rehabilitation classes.

We heard a malicious destruction case. A mason with a long unpronounceable Italian name was accused of knocking down the brick walls he had constructed at a new condominium complex because the contractor had fired him halfway through the job. The prosecutor, a young female assistant district attorney, built her case entirely on the testimony of the contractor, corroborated by two witnesses, that the mason had cursed and uttered oblique threats when he was let go, and had thrust his arm from the window of his pickup truck and extended his middle finger as he drove away. Her implied argument, simply, was: Who else could have done it?

Nobody had seen him at the scene of the crime since the afternoon he was fired, the only point the defense attorney bothered to emphasize in his cross-examination of the witnesses.

When both sides rested, Judge Ropek said that he, for one, still retained reasonable doubt. Not guilty. It was the correct verdict.

The whole thing took less than an hour.

When the court recessed around eleven, twenty-five or thirty citizens had had their lives significantly altered by decisions rendered in the Northampton District Court. About a dozen couldn't drive automobiles for sixty days. Another dozen or so no longer needed to report to probation officers. A few would soon be arrested for probation violations. One Italian stonemason found himself relieved of both worry and a few thousand dollars in legal fees.

Daniel McCloud was still jiggling his leg and waiting.

I went outside for a cigarette. I wondered how Daniel had endured the weekend without what he called his medicine. I hoped his case would come up before the lunch recess.

I thought about what I had witnessed during the previous two hours. Justice. Routine, boring, repetitive justice had been dispensed evenhandedly by Judge Anthony Ropek. In the course of a week, justice would be meted out hundreds of times in this courtroom, as it would in dozens of other courtrooms across the state.

My law practice rarely requires me to perform the peculiar formalities of courtroom routines. Most of my work is done by telephone or in conference in a lawyer's office. Most of my practice is civil and probate, and you can judge the effectiveness of a civil or probate lawyer by his success in resolving issues before they find their way into a courtroom. It's the law of give-and-take, compromise, negotiation. It's my niche, and I'm pretty good at it.

Criminal law is different. The state, not a private citizen, is the adversary. The ground rules are more formalized, less flexible. Behind the state stand massive bureaucracies, enormous budgets, up-to-date technology. Behind the accused stands only a lone attorney, more often than not one who has been appointed by the state, and the presumption of innocence.

It usually turns out to be a pretty fair contest. The state bears the burden of proof. The presumption of innocence is a powerful ally.

On those relatively rare occasions when I find myself handling a criminal case, I inevitably recognize it as somehow more important. My client stands to lose not just some money, or his house, or custody of his children. Criminal clients go to prison when their lawyers screw up. Sometimes, because they are in fact guilty as charged, they go to prison even when their lawyers don't screw up. Under this system, remarkably few innocent people are imprisoned—although a remarkably large number of guilty people go free. Still, I, for one, never can avoid the feeling that I've screwed up whenever one of my clients goes to prison. Even when they're guilty, I always feel that I should have been able to get a "not guilty" verdict.

There's a big difference between "not guilty" and "innocent."

What would soon happen on that muggy Monday morning in July in the old Northampton courthouse, I knew, was the beginning of an intricate process that could land Daniel McCloud in M.C.I. Cedar Junction for fifteen years. What actually would happen would depend more than it should on me.

That Daniel did in fact grow marijuana in his garden, that he was therefore a guilty man by every definition except the one that counted—the due process of the law—did not affect my attitude toward his case. The presumption of innocence and the right to counsel—only those things were relevant.

If he'd been selling the stuff—not something the state needed to prove—I'd have felt differently about it. But, having agreed to take his case, I still would have done my best to get him off. That's the system, and it's not a bad one.

I flicked away my cigarette butt and went back into the courthouse. As I shouldered my way through the crowded lobby I felt a hand on my arm. I turned. It was the ADA who had unsuccessfully prosecuted the bricklayer. "You're Mr. McCloud's counsel?" she said.

I nodded. "Brady Coyne."

"Joan Redlich. Here." She handed me a sheet of paper.

"What's this?"

"The police report. You're entitled to it."

"Yes. Thanks. I'll want a copy of the warrant, too."

She smiled quickly. "You'll have it, Mr. Coyne."

She turned and headed into the courtroom. I followed her in and resumed my seat. I skimmed through the police report. It was written in the peculiarly stilted language policemen insist on using, on their theory, I assume, that it makes them sound highly educated.

To me, it always sounds like somebody trying to sound highly educated.

The report was signed by Sgt. Richard Oakley, Wilson Falls P.D.

Sergeant Oakley had written that the Wilson Falls police, acting upon a proper warrant, did on the afternoon of seven July confiscate an estimated fifty pounds or more of marijuana from the backyard garden of one Daniel McCloud, citizen of Wilson Falls. They did, pursuant to a search of the premises, also confiscate cigarette papers, a scale, a box of plastic bags, fifteen smoking pipes of various manufacture, and a cigarette rolling machine. They did consequently place the suspect, said Daniel McCloud, under arrest, recite to him his Miranda rights, handcuff him, and escort him to the jailhouse, where they did finger-print and book him.

It was all pretty much the way Daniel had told it, except less eloquent.

A few minutes later the side door opened and Judge Ropek reentered. We all rose briefly, and then sat.

"Daniel McCloud," intoned the clerk.

Daniel stood, and the officer opened the swinging door to let him out of the dock. I went down front and Daniel met me there.

"You okay?" I whispered.

"No," he said. He glanced around, then muttered, "Bastard."

I followed his gaze. Standing stiffly against the side wall was a large uniformed policeman. He was staring at Daniel. He stood six-three or -four with the bulk to match. He had the bristly haircut and sunburned neck of a marine drill instructor. "Oakley?" I whispered to Daniel.

"Aye. Him."

"He's interested in his case," I said.

"He's interested in me," said Daniel.

The clerk read the charges. Possession of Class D marijuana, possession with intent to distribute, and traf-ficking.

The judge arched his eyebrows, then looked toward the prosecution table. "Trafficking, Ms. Redlich?"

Joan Redlich stood up and stepped toward the prose-cutor's table. Her black hair was twisted up into a bun. I guessed it would fall halfway down her back when it was unpinned. She wore dark-rimmed tinted glasses low on her nose, a gray suit that disguised her figure, and low heels. She was slim and young and, in spite of her best efforts, pretty.

Female lawyers have told me that they dress for the judge. They have different wardrobes, different hairstyles, different cosmetics, which they adapt to the situation. Some judges—His Dirty Old Honors, the lawyers call them—like to see a little leg, a hint of cleavage, eye makeup. It disposes them favorably to the client's case. Others—especially female judges—resent it if the lawyers don't look as shapeless and sexless as they do in their black gowns.

Female lawyers resent the hell out of this kind of patent sexism. But they don't ignore it. It's an edge, if you read it right, they tell me.

Redlich tucked a stray strand of hair over her ear. She leaned toward the microphone that was wired to the tape recorder that preserved the proceedings and rendered obsolete the court stenographer. "Cultivation, Your Honor," she said. "He was growing it in his garden. The estimate is seventy pounds."

Ropek frowned, then nodded. I didn't like the looks of that frown. "Recommendation?"

She asked for a half-millon-dollar surety bond. Not unexpected. Since Reagan, all the courts have been trying to convert the drug cases that come before them into moral lessons.

"Mr. McCloud?" said the judge, looking from Daniel to me.

"Brady Coyne, Your Honor," I said into my microphone.

"Welcome, Mr. Coyne. Go ahead."

"I ask the court to release Mr. McCloud on personal recognizance, Your Honor. He has roots deep in the community. He's resided in Wilson Falls for the past twenty years. He owns property and runs a business there. He's a Vietnam veteran, Special Forces, and he's in poor health."

The judge peered at me for a moment, then nodded. He looked to the probation table. "Probation?" he said.

"One prior, Judge," said one of the officers. He stood and went to the bench, where he handed a folder to the judge. Judge Ropek glanced at it, then handed it back.

Then he looked at Daniel. "Two hundred thousand dollars surety bond," he said.

Daniel grabbed my arm. "I don't have that kind of money," he whispered.

"You need twenty thousand cash," I told him. "Can you raise it?"

He nodded. "Twenty grand. Okay. Yes."

We then argued about the date for the probable-cause hearing. Redlich asked for a month to give them time to process all the evidence. I asked for a week, citing the stress of waiting on Daniel's health. Judge Ropek set it for ten days hence, a small victory for the good guys.

Before the court officer took Daniel away, he gave me a phone number and told me to talk to Cammie Russell. She'd get the money.

And as I turned to head out of the courtroom, Joan Redlich handed me a copy of the search warrant. I thanked her and stuffed it into my attaché case along with the police report.

I called Cammie Russell from one of the pay phones

in the courthouse lobby. She had a soft voice with a hint of the Smoky Mountains in it. She said she'd be there in an hour. I told her I'd meet her outside the front door.

She actually arrived in about forty minutes. She was tall and slim in her white jeans and orange blouse. She had cocoa butter skin and black eyes. Her hair hung in a long, loose braid down the middle of her back. Her high cheekbones and small nose reminded me of a young Lena Horne. There was a Cherokee Indian somewhere in her ancestry. I guessed her age at twenty-five, but I figured she had looked the same way since she turned thirteen and would still look as good at fifty.

Then she smiled, and I amended my first impression. She looked *better* than a young Lena Horne.

She held her hand to me. "Cammie Russell," she said.

"Brady Coyne."

"How is Daniel?"

I shrugged. "I don't know how he usually is. I'd say confinement doesn't suit him."

"I can see you're a master of understatement, Mr. Coyne. He must be climbing the walls. Can we get him now?"

"If you brought enough money we can."

She held up the briefcase she was carrying and nodded.

An hour later Cammie Russell and I were eating ham-and-cheese sandwiches and sipping coffee on the deck behind Daniel's house in Wilson Falls. Daniel was slouched in a deck chair with his eyes closed, sucking steadily on a stick of cannabis. His leg no longer jiggled.

.

3

The deck across the back of Daniel's house looked out over a meadow that stretched toward a bluff above the Connecticut River. It had once been a tobacco farm, he told me, and he'd lived there since '73, when he retired from the Army. He rented a trailer and ran a bait and tackle shop for the ten years or so that it took him to realize that he'd never have to go back to the jungles. Finally he managed to accumulate some money, so he bought the land and the shop and built his house and, a few years later, Cammie's studio down next to the river.

Daniel's house featured angled cedar sheathing and glass and brick on the outside, and skylights and fireplaces and vaulted ceilings and massive beams on the inside. He told me he designed it himself, and he and some of his old army buddies did most of the work. It took them a couple of years to complete. The entire back was floor-to-ceiling glass that opened onto the big deck and overlooked the river.

The house was elegant and modern. It could have been a *Better Homes and Gardens* model. It contradicted every impression I had formed of Daniel McCloud.

After Daniel had sucked his second joint down to a quarter-inch nub, he stood up and said he needed a shower. He walked into the house.

"Is he stoned?" I said to Cammie.

She laughed. "He never gets stoned. It just eases his pain. It's the only thing that will." She was sitting up on the deck rail. "Daniel's death on drugs. That's why this business is so unfair. He saw a lot of men get killed over there because they were wasted and forgot to be afraid. It wasn't until he got back and tried every legal medicine they prescribed that he came to grass. Brian Sweeney put him on to it. The two of them have been trying to get help from the government. Mainly, they'd like to get the law to allow them to have marijuana legally."

"No way," I said.

She nodded. "'No farkin' way,' as Daniel would say. So he grows his own."

"Except they ripped up his garden," I said. "What'll he do?"

She shrugged. "He's got a little stashed away. Not much. I don't know how long it'll last him. I don't think he could make it without his medicine. In or out of prison."

"He can always buy it," I said.

Cammie's head jerked up. "Daniel?" She smiled. "You don't know Daniel. He would never—*never*—give money to a drug dealer."

"He's obviously a sick man."

"Wouldn't matter." She shrugged. "Can you get him off?"

"I don't know," I said. "There are plenty of mitigating circumstances in this case. But unless the prosecution screws it up, the facts will be hard to challenge. I mean, they don't have to prove he was selling it, and he *was* growing the stuff. So far the police appear to have gone by the book. If it goes to trial we'll probably have to give them a guilty plea. That'll be our only chance of keeping Daniel out of prison."

"If?"

"The next step is the probable-cause hearing," I said. "The prosecutor will have to demonstrate that she has enough evidence to justify a trial. If it gets to trial, I'll ask a friend of mine, a lawyer with a lot of experience at this sort of thing, to come aboard."

"You're not going to abandon him?" said Cammie.

I shook my head.

"Because," she continued, "I can tell he trusts you. He doesn't trust many people."

"I won't abandon him."

She cocked her head at me. "You were probably wondering about us."

I shrugged. "None of my business."

"Maybe it is," she said. "Maybe it relates to Daniel's case. Maybe you can use it. I mean, he really does hate drugs. What they do to people. Despises drug dealers. You should probably know, so you can judge. I doubt Daniel would tell you."

I nodded. "Okay."

She nodded and stared off toward the river. The Connecticut's a big broad river out there in the valley. It flows slow and deep through the old tobacco bottom land. It's not a trout stream, but bass and pike live there, and shad push up from the ocean every spring to spawn, and just looking at it gave me the urge to go fishing.

"He saved my life," said Cammie softly.

"Daniel?"

"Yes. I was this overachiever from a little mountain town outside of Knoxville. The youngest of eight. I had four sisters and three brothers, two of whom got killed in Vietnam. My momma sang choir in the Baptist church. So did I. One of my teachers got me into Smith College on a scholarship. I was going to be a great artist." She glanced at me and smiled softly. "I wasn't ready. I was homesick, I was over my head academically, I had no friends. I made some bad acquaintances." She shrugged. "Three months after I started my freshman year I was hooking in Springfield for coke money, living with a pimp, scared to death. Daniel found me and brought me here. I was eighteen. He got me straightened out. We lived in a trailer for a while. Eventually Daniel built me a studio and told me to just paint and cherish my life."

"What happened to the pimp?"

"I don't know." She shrugged. "This all happened years ago. I used to wake up from dreaming that he'd come for me. I haven't had that dream in a while."

"What about that policeman?"

"Oakley?"

I nodded.

"Well, he was the one who arrested Daniel, of course. Oakley's had it in for us from the start."

"How do you mean?"

Cammie gazed out at the river. "Small things," she said. "A ticket for parking in a handicapped zone, when the tire was barely touching the line. He stopped Daniel once in the middle of the afternoon, made him get out of the car and go through a bunch of drunk-driving exercises right beside the road, with all our neighbors driving by to watch. Oakley keeps showing up in the supermarket or the post office or the drugstore when I'm there, just kind of watching me with this spooky smile on his face. I'll turn around, and he'll be there, looking at me." She shrugged. "I don't know. It's no one thing. Maybe we're just paranoid about Oakley. It's a small town . . ."

"Are you afraid of him?"

Cammie closed her eyes for a moment. When she opened them, she turned to look at me and said, "Yes. I guess I am. Daniel's not afraid of him. But he worries about me. And now this . . ."

"The arrest."

She nodded.

We fell silent for a minute. Then I said, "Was Daniel growing marijuana when you met him?"

"Yes. He has this terrible raw, weeping rash on his back. From the Agent Orange. He doesn't talk about his pain, and when you're with him you'd never know how miserable he is."

"He seemed pretty miserable when I saw him in jail."

She nodded. "That's because he didn't have his medicine. It's worst at night. When he's sleeping he moans and thrashes around as if he was having one continuous nightmare." She looked up at me. "We don't sleep together. I mean, we're together, we . . . we're lovers, we make love . . . but he can't sleep with anybody else in the room, and I can't sleep with him anyway, because he's so restless. I sleep in my studio. It's down there." She gestured off to the left toward the river. I glimpsed the reflection of sun off glass through the trees. "It's got a bedroom, kitchen, living room, bath, and the whole top floor's a studio. Great light. I do watercolors, mostly, and— Oh, hi."

I turned. Daniel was standing there. He had shaved and changed his clothes.

Cammie smiled at me. "He's always doing that. Sneaking up on me." To him she said, "I suppose you were eavesdropping."

He twitched his shoulder. "I heard most of it."

"Okay?" she said.

Another shrug. "Brady's got to know."

"I've got a question," I said to Cammie.

"What?"

"Were you ever arrested?"

"Me?"

I nodded.

"Oh," she said. "I get it. If they knew I was a hooker, that I was a drug addict, it could go against Daniel."

"Unlikely," I said, "but it's possible."

She stared off toward the river for a moment, then said, "Twice. They pulled me in twice. Boomer got me off both times."

"Boomer?"

"Her pimp," said Daniel.

"There'll be a record of it, if it occurs to them to check," I said.

"It would be ironic as hell," said Cammie. "I mean, it was Daniel who got me out of that life."

"Well," I said, "one of the things Daniel has going for him is that he's a good citizen. But . . ."

"But living with me makes it look different," she finished.

I nodded. "If you look at it that way. Which is possibly the way the prosecution could try to make a jury look at it." I sighed. "Anyway, this is all a little premature. We've got the probable-cause hearing first, and we can try to make some good things happen there."

"Like what?" said Daniel.

"Like tainted evidence, improper warrant. Maybe all they got from your garden was tomato plants. If they ended up with less than fifty pounds of marijuana plants, they'll have to drop the trafficking charge, and that would be a very good thing."

Daniel smiled. "It was a big garden, and the crop was getting ripe. It was supposed to be my year's supply. That's probably why they waited until now to do it. So they got their fifty pounds."

"We'll see," I said. "For now, the ball's in their court."

"In that case," said Daniel, "let's go fishing."

I started to object that I had to get back to the office. But I caught myself. Hell, it was *my* office.

So I found a rumpled change of clothes in the trunk of my car, and Daniel and I strolled down to the river. We did it Daniel's way. No fly rods, delicate hand-tied flies, English reels, neoprene waders, bulging vests. We cut birch poles, captured some crickets for bait, and hauled a mess of panfish out of the sluggishly flowing Connecticut River. It was barefoot-boy-with-canepole fishing, and it harkened me back to the days when time was my most abundant resource and I squandered most of it aimlessly on the banks of muddy ponds.

We stopped and sat and smoked frequently, me my Winstons and Daniel his hand-rolled joints. We talked a little, gazed upon the river, and watched the birds. And we became friends.

When we had enough bluegills and perch for a meal, Daniel filleted them all with a wicked little blade that he kept sheathed against his calf.

Afterward, Daniel fried the panfish fillets, and he and Cammie and I ate them with steamed brown rice and sliced tomatoes and a bottle of what even I recognized as an excellent Chardonnay.

Later we sat out on the big deck behind Daniel's house to watch the sky grow dark. We sipped coffee and listened to Daniel's collection of blues tapes. Sonny Terry. John Lee Hooker. Brownie McGhee. Son House. Muddy Waters. Doc Reese. Mississippi John Hurt. Skip James. Lightnin' Hopkins. Howlin' Wolf. Jimmy Reed. Daniel and Cammie and I tapped our feet and made harmonica noises, and it was nearly midnight when the three of us walked around front to my car.

I told Daniel I'd see him in ten days for the probable-cause hearing.

"You've got to keep him out of prison," said Cammie.

"Our chances are excellent," I said.

Daniel shrugged. "They got my garden," he said. "Either way, I'm screwed."

I looked at him. "You can always buy some grass," I said.

"No," said Daniel. "I wouldn't do that. Sweeney might, but not me."

"I told you," said Cammie. "Daniel's death on drugs."

I called Charlie McDevitt the next morning from my office. "Daniel McCloud is quite amazing," I told him.

I heard Charlie chuckle. "I knew you'd like him."

"We went fishing, and it took me right back to when I was about eight," I said. "Him, too, I think. We were like a pair of kids. Except Daniel is about the most resourceful man in the woods that I've ever known."

"He survived six years in the jungle, you know," said Charlie.

"Well, he'd never survive prison. When I saw him in jail, he was like a caged animal, and I don't think it was just the fact that he didn't have his . . . his medicine. I mean, the marijuana eases his pain. But freedom nourishes him."

"He's a very complicated man," said Charlie. "Even though he doesn't like to show it."

"A little paranoid, though. He thinks it's personal with the cop who arrested him."

"Maybe it is," said Charlie. "Cops aren't immune from personal motives."

"Maybe so," I said. "Anyway, I like him a lot. He's very stoic. But it's pretty clear that he suffers a lot."

"I can imagine," said Charlie. "So what do you think? Have they got the goods on him?"

"It looks bad, truthfully. I'm not sure what I can do for him."

"You've gotta keep him out of prison, Brady," said Charlie. "It would kill him."

"What worries me," I said, "is that not having his medicine could kill him no matter where he is."

4

Ten days later, Daniel, Cammie Russell, and I were sitting in Judge Anthony Ropek's courtroom while he and his clerk worked their way through the morning's probation cases. Sergeant Oakley was there, too, standing stiffly in the back, staring in our direction.

It was a little after ten when the clerk intoned, "Daniel McCloud."

Daniel followed me through the gate to the defense table. Joan Redlich, the same ADA who had handled the arraignment for the state, moved to the prosecutor's table.

The judge peered down at her. "Is the Commonwealth ready?"

She glanced in our direction, then turned to the judge. She cleared her throat, leaned to the microphone, then said, "The Commonwealth moves to dismiss, Your Honor."

Judge Ropek frowned for an instant, then turned to me. "Mr. Coyne?"

"May I have a moment, Your Honor?"

He nodded. "Go ahead."

I hadn't expected the state to move for dismissal. It was more than I'd dared hope for. But I didn't have the luxury of exulting in our good luck. I needed to decide whether to move for a dismissal with prejudice. If prejudice was granted, it would prevent the state from ever reopening its case against Daniel. With a simple dismissal, they could try it again. The problem was, I'd have to convince Judge Ropek that there had actually been prejudice in Daniel's arrest. Daniel thought it had been personal with Sergeant Oakley. I doubted that I could convert Daniel's paranoia into an argument for prejudice that would convince the judge.

The other factor to consider was Joan Redlich's failure to request a continuance, which would have indicated simply that the state needed more time to prepare its case. She had asked for a dismissal, not a continuance. I guessed that they didn't have the evidence to prosecute the case.

I had no grounds for prejudice.

I looked up at Judge Ropek. "Thank you, Your Honor," I said. "No argument with the motion."

He looked back to Redlich and beckoned her with a crooked forefinger. "Approach," he growled.

She went up to the bench. I sidled up next to her.

"What the hell is going on?" said the judge to her in a harsh whisper.

"Apparently there's a problem with the evidence, Judge," she said.

"Apparently?"

She shrugged.

He looked at me. "You know anything about this?"

"No, Your Honor. But we'll take it."

"Don't blame you, Mr. Coyne." He shooed us away with the back of his hand.

We returned to our tables.

"Mr. McCloud, you are free to go," said Judge Ropek to Daniel. "The Commonwealth apologizes for your inconvenience."

Daniel blinked at him and nodded.

"Thank you, Your Honor," I said. I picked up my briefcase. "Come on," I said to Daniel.

I walked up the aisle and out of the courtroom. Daniel followed behind me. Cammie had grabbed his arm. We stopped in the lobby.

"What happened?" said Daniel.

I shrugged. "Somebody must've screwed up the evidence. You sure they didn't just get tomato plants or something?"

He smiled. "They got some damn good weed, Brady."

"Well," I said, "it's peculiar. But let's not complain. I only—"

I felt a hand on my arm. I turned and saw Joan Redlich. "Can I speak to you for a second, Mr. Coyne?" she said.

"Sure." I turned to Daniel and Cammie. "Be with you in a minute."

"We'll wait outside," said Daniel.

I turned to the ADA. "What's up?" I said.

"You tell me."

"Don't look at me," I said. "Surprised me as much as it did you."

She rolled her eyes. "Sure."

"Look," I said. "If you think I pulled a string, you're giving me more credit than I deserve."

She narrowed her eyes. "I figured, a fancy Boston lawyer . . ."

"You figured wrong. I'm not that fancy, and I thought you had a decent case, to tell you the truth." I smiled at her. "I was looking forward to it."

She did not smile. "Decent, yeah. I had a helluva good case. There were sixty-two pounds of marijuana plants in those trash bags they pulled out of that garden, according to the lab report. The warrant was okay and the search followed it perfectly. Look," she said. "I've got nothing against Mr. McCloud, okay? There's no evidence that he was dealing the stuff. I know he's sick. I mean, I've got plenty of bad guys to prosecute. I doubt if Daniel McCloud is a bad guy." She cocked her head and arched her eyebrows at me.

"He's actually a pretty good guy," I said.

"Regardless, there was no way we would've lost that trial. No matter how good you are."

"I'm pretty good. It would've been interesting."

"I don't think Daniel McCloud belongs in prison," she said. "I would have argued my ass off for a guilty verdict, Mr. Coyne. And I would've got it. And you probably would've requested a suspended sentence with a long probation, community service, and proper health care, and, between the two of us, I might not've objected too strenuously. The poor bastard deserves some help, and I think a lot of our vets've been getting screwed. But, dammit, I just don't like having the rug pulled out from under me, and I was wondering if you could help me out."

I held up both hands. "This discussion isn't really appropriate, Ms. Redlich," I said with a smile.

"Ah, come off it. We're just a couple of lawyers here."

"Well, as one lawyer to another, I haven't got the foggiest idea of what happened."

"You've got friends in high places, though, huh?"

I thought of Charlie. "Don't we all?"

"I busted my butt on this case, okay?" she said. "And they wait till yesterday to tell me to dump it?"

"Well," I said, "I don't blame you for being upset. But I can't help you. I don't know what happened."

"Would you tell me if you did?"

I nodded. "Maybe."

She peered quizzically at me for a moment, then shrugged. "Well, it was fun being your adversary, and if I didn't have a caseload that'd choke a hippo I'd get to the bottom of this. But, screw it. I do, so I guess I won't." She smiled and held her hand to me, and I grasped it.

"If it's any consolation," I said, "I think justice was done in there this morning."

She grinned crookedly. "Yeah. Whatever that means."

She turned and strode back into the courtroom and I went out into the summer heat.

I squinted into the sunlight as I tapped a Winston from my pack and lit it. Daniel and Cammie were sitting on a bench by the front entrance. I went over and sat with them.

"I could use a smoke," said Daniel, jerking his head at my cigarette.

"Not here you couldn't," I said.

"Just kidding."

"From now on, you've got to be careful," I told him.

"I can't live without my medicine," he said.

"I understand."

"What happened in there?" said Cammie.

"I don't know. The ADA didn't know, either. I gather her boss ordered her to dump the case."

"But why?"

"A small mystery that doesn't need to concern us. Daniel's free, all charges dropped for now. Let's be grateful."

"For now?" repeated Cammie.

"They could reopen the case."

"But it was dismissed."

"Without prejudice," I said. "Meaning there's no admission that they did anything wrong. But look. I don't think we have anything to worry about. This is one for the good guys."

"Do I get my weed back?" said Daniel.

I looked at him. He managed to withhold his grin for several seconds. I punched his shoulder. "The Wilson Falls P.D. is probably divvying it up right now," I said. "Maybe they divvied it up yesterday, and that's why the case got dropped."

"Wouldn't surprise me," he said.

We were strolling to the parking lot when Daniel suddenly stopped. I turned to follow his gaze. Sergeant Richard Oakley was leaning back against a Wilson Falls police cruiser. His arms were folded across his chest, and behind his reflector sunglasses he appeared to be staring at Cammie. He was grinning, baring his teeth.

She grabbed Daniel's arm. "Come on," she said.

Daniel remained there for another moment, glaring at the policeman. Then he shrugged, and we continued to my car.

"You can expect them to be watching you," I told Daniel as we drove back to his place. "They figured they had a good arrest. These things do not make policemen happy. You've got to be careful."

"Not them," he said. "Just him. Oakley. And anyway, he wasn't watching me. He was watching Cammie."

I stopped off at Daniel's house for coffee. Cammie offered to make lunch for me, but I told her I had to get back to the office. We sat at the table in Daniel's sun-drenched ultramodern kitchen. "I meant it about being careful," I said to him. "I don't know what happened in court today, but it's for sure that they'd love to try again."

Daniel shrugged. He had just stubbed out a joint. "I can't live without my medicine."

"So what are you going to do?"

"I don't know." He stood up. "Brady, I've got something for you. Wait here."

He walked out of the room. I lifted my eyebrows at Cammie. She shrugged.

He was back in a minute. He was carrying a box, the kind that holds a ream of typing paper. It was heavily taped along its seams. He put it on the table in front of me.

"What's this?" I said.

"My book."

"Daniel . . ." began Cammie.

"It's time, lass," he said. He sat down beside me. "You're a lawyer. You can handle it for me."

"You want it published?"

"Aye."

"You need an agent, not a lawyer, Daniel."

He shrugged. "Whatever."

"You want me to find an agent for you?"

"Yes."

I smiled. "Daniel, you understand—"

"That everybody and his sister has written a book they think is going to make them rich and famous. Yes, I know that. I'm not interested in getting rich or famous. That's not why I wrote it."

I nodded. I thought I understood. Daniel was haunted by mighty demons. His book was his exorcism.

"I'm using a pen name," he added. "This book isn't for me."

"What kind of book is it?"

He gave me an understated shrug. "A story, I guess."

"I mean, a novel? A memoir?"

"Just a story."

"Can I look at it?"

He peered at me for a moment, then shook his head. "No," he said. "It's all ready to send off. Can you just find someone to send it off to?"

"Sure," I said. "I'll see what I can do."

I got back to the office around two in the afternoon. Julie greeted me with a stack of messages. I clutched the box with Daniel's manuscript in it against my chest. "Don't pester me," I said. "I haven't had any lunch."

"Poor baby."

"Have you?"

She looked at me and rolled her eyes.

"I'm sorry," I said. "Of course you haven't. Let me make a quick call and then I'll run out for sandwiches."

I went into my office. Julie followed me. "How'd it go this morning?" she said.

"The prosecutor moved for dismissal."

Julie sat down. "No shit."

I sat, too. "No shit indeed."

"Why?"

I shrugged. "Beats me."

"Well, that's good, huh?"

"It certainly is. I mean, they would've presented their evidence and I would've moved for dismissal on the ground that their evidence was insufficient. I would've challenged the warrant, the reliability of their informants. All the usual things. But my motion would've been denied, and the judge would've found probable cause, and the ADA would've taken the case to the grand jury for an indictment. Which they would've gotten. And on to trial."

She gave me her stunning Irish smile. "You're a helluva lawyer, Brady Coyne. The prosecutor takes one look at you and figures it's a lost cause."

"Yeah," I said, "I guess that's what happened."

"Look," she said. "You want tuna?"

"I said I'd get them."

"Hey, you're the victorious attorney. I'll go out. You watch the phone."

"Tomato and lettuce with the tuna," I said. "On a bulky roll. Barbecued chips, dill pickle, ice-cold Pepsi."

"Don't press your luck, fella."

After Julie left I called Charlie, as I had promised him I would. When Shirley, his secretary, put me through, he said, "Well?"

"The Commonwealth moved to dismiss."

He was quiet for so long that I said, "Charlie? You there?"

"I'm here. What the hell happened?"

"Come off it," I said.

"What are you talking about?"

"I just don't understand why you made us go through the arraignment and then the hearing first. It would've been a helluva lot easier on all of us if—"

"Brady," said Charlie, "what the Christ are you talking about?"

"Don't give me your bullshit, old buddy. You pulled some strings. I'm calling to say thanks on Daniel McCloud's behalf."

"I didn't do anything."

"Hey, I understand that your overdeveloped concept of ethics prevents you from admitting it. But thanks anyway."

"Honest," he said. "I don't have that kind of pull with the Commonwealth. I don't work those streets. I'm just a D.O.J. drudge, one of Uncle Sam's soldiers, remember?"

"Listen, Charlie—"

"Brady, believe me, it wasn't me. I wish it was. If I'd thought there was anything I could do for you—for Daniel—I would've done it. But I didn't. You don't know what happened?"

"Maybe it *was* a fuckup with the evidence, then," I said.

"Probably. Those things happen."

"So I rescind my thanks."

"In which case," said Charlie, "I am absolved from having to say 'You're welcome.'"

"Daniel has written a book," I told Charlie.

"Daniel?"

"Yep. And I'm to find him an agent."

"What kind of book?"

"I don't know. He won't say."

Charlie chuckled. "Everybody's got a story these days, huh?"

5

Later that afternoon I left my office and strolled across the square to the Boston Public Library, where I copied out a dozen phone numbers from a writer's directory. Then I returned to the office and began calling New York literary agencies. They all wanted the same thing—a cover letter detailing the author's credentials and something they called a "chapter outline," which they explained was a brief narrative summary of the book's plot. Until they had a chance to review an outline, they all informed me, they wouldn't touch a manuscript from an anonymous and unpublished writer.

As far as I knew, Daniel had no credentials. And he had given me no outline.

I called him that night. "Credentials?" he said.

"Credits. Things that you've had published."

"Nay," he said. "I have no credentials. Unless you can count the demolition handbook I helped revise."

"I doubt if that would count."

"I was really a technical adviser on it anyway," he said.

"How about making an outline for me?"

"Just find someone who'll read the book, Brady."

"They don't seem interested in reading it."

"They'll be interested in this one."

"Daniel," I said, "do you know what the odds are on this book getting published?"

"I know all about long odds," he said quietly.

"The publishing world is a different kind of jungle," I said.

"Just find someone willing to read it. They'll take it."

I sighed. "Well, I'll keep trying. But no guarantees."

As I lay in bed that night, I thought I remembered having read in my alumni magazine that one of my Yale Law classmates had become a literary agent. Damned if I could remember his name, however.

It kept me awake half the night, which didn't help.

Charlie remembered. "Al Coleman," he said instantly when I called him the next morning. "Little guy with glasses. Looked like Woody Allen. Used to beat the shit out of me at handball. We kept in touch for a while after we got out of school. He went to work for Uncle right after Yale. Over at State, I think it was. Al was a pretty rigid guy. Couldn't take the bullshit, all the nuances and ambiguities that are more or less part of government work. Had this overdeveloped concept of the law, justice." He paused. "Not unlike you, in fact."

"Or you, for that matter," I said.

"I guess Yale bred that into us," said Charlie. "Anyway, Coleman quit after a few years, set up his own practice.

Again, kind of like you. A little of this, a little of that. Al and I lost touch, but I heard some kiss-and-tell writer hired him to defend a lawsuit, and he won it, so she retained him, and he ended up making a bundle representing her. Eventually he gave up his practice and set up an agency. As I recall, he specializes in ghostwritten celebrity biographies."

"Al Coleman," I mused. "Sounds familiar. Did I know him?"

"He came out to our place a few times," said Charlie, referring to the ramshackle house near the water that he and I rented while we were in New Haven. "You were with Gloria in those days, pretty oblivious to anybody else."

"Used to bring that tall blonde?" I said. "About six inches taller than him?"

"That's the guy. It figures you'd remember the lady."

"I remember her well. I wasn't that oblivious."

"Well, that's what Al Coleman does now. Represents writers." Charlie paused. "So you're really going to try to help Daniel, huh?"

"I promised him I would."

"I hear that getting an agent is about as hard as getting a publisher."

"I've heard that, too."

"Well, give Al Coleman a try. Sing the Whiffenpoof song to him. Maybe he'll give it a look."

"Yeah, I guess I will," I said. "I wonder what happened to the blonde?"

"She got old," said Charlie. "Like the rest of us."

I slipped over to the BPL at lunchtime. The directory

listed the Coleman Literary Agency on lower Fifth Avenue in New York City. The heart of the publishing district.

Back at my desk, I dialed their number. A sexy female voice answered.

"Al Coleman, please," I said.

"Who should I say is calling?"

"Brady Coyne. We're friends."

"One moment, sir."

I was treated to two minutes of Mozart while I waited on hold. Then she came back on and said, "Mr. Coyne, what was it you wanted?"

Fair enough, I thought. I hadn't remembered Al Coleman, and he didn't remember me. "Tell Al," I said, "that he used to come down to the house that Charlie McDevitt and I rented while we were all at Yale Law together. Tell him he used to bring a beautiful blonde with him. Tell him I have a manuscript that I want to give him first shot at. Because we're old friends."

"Oh," she said. She started to say something, then stopped herself. "Well, okay," she said instead. "Hang on a minute."

More Mozart. Then, "Hey, Brady. How've you been?"

"Cut the shit, Al," I said. "Charlie had to remind me of you, and you don't remember me."

He laughed. It was a good, genuine laugh. "I *do* remember Charlie. And that shack you guys rented. I remember you, too, except your name failed to ring a bell. I remember the vats of fish chowder you guys'd cook up and all the beer. I used to play handball with Charlie."

"He said you were good."

"Nah. Charlie was bad, that's all. You and Charlie used to claim that you made that chowder from fish you caught yourselves."

"True. We never told you what kind of fish they were, though."

"What, eels?"

"Among other unmentionables," I said.

He chuckled. "So you've written a book, huh?"

"Not me. One of my clients has written one, and he's asked me to find an agent for it. I thought of you."

"Tell me about it."

"I haven't read it."

"Send me an outline. I'll give it a look."

"No outline. He refuses to do one. Says the book speaks for itself. He's a funny guy. Very shy. Wants to use a pseudonym. He's a Vietnam vet, got himself doused with Agent Orange over there."

"Well, what've we got? A novel or what?"

"I don't know. A story, he calls it."

"Christ," he muttered. "How'm I supposed to take a book, you can't even tell me what kind of book it is?"

"I understand."

I heard Al sigh. "The market's real soft on Vietnam stuff just now, Brady."

"I don't even know if it's a Vietnam book. I was just hoping you'd look at it. I know you can't guarantee anything."

"You have any idea how many people are writing books these days?"

"Too many, I guess." I hesitated. "Listen," I said, "if

you could just glance at it, maybe tell me if it's worth anything. You know, if I should just tell Daniel to forget it."

He was silent for a long moment. Then he said, "I guess I could look at it. That's what the old school tie is all about, huh?"

"I appreciate it, Al," I said.

"Send it down."

"I will."

"It'll take me a few weeks to get back to you."

"Fine. Understood." I hesitated. "Hey, Al?"

"Yeah?"

"What ever happened to that blonde?"

"The one I used to bring to your parties?"

"That one."

"I married her."

"Yeah?"

"Yeah. She's the one who answers the phone here. You just talked to her. We've got four kids. What about you?"

"Me?"

"Yeah. You used to have a knockout brunette with you. I can almost remember her name."

"Gloria," I said.

"Right. What happened to her?"

"I married her."

"Oh."

"Yes. We have two boys. Divorced eleven years ago."

"Well, I'm sorry."

"Sometimes I am, too."

6

Al Coleman called me back two weeks later. "I really got my hands full here," he said. "I hardly ever take on a new client. I'm trying to avoid hiring anybody. It's just me and Bonnie. A two-person office, that's how I want it."

"Me, too," I said. "Maybe Yale bred that into us. The lone-wolf mentality. Does this mean—?"

"I handle everything myself," he interrupted. "Personal attention. My writers always know who they're dealing with. They appreciate it that way. I've got a few big name writers, and several good solid pros. They take all my time, keep me as busy as I want to be. It'd take something really special for me to bring another writer aboard, especially someone who's got no track record. Something like what you sent me, I just have a policy against even looking at stuff like that, and I'm afraid I'm pretty closed-minded about unproven writers. Do you understand?"

"Sure. That's fine. I appreciate your looking at it, anyway. So what did you—"

"I mean," Al went on quickly, "we do have to keep bringing new blood into the literary world and all that. Every bestselling author in history started with a first book. But a little mom-and-pop operation like mine, I just don't have the luxury of beating my brains out trying to sell something that's not going to make anybody any money. That's just how it's gotta be. Big agencies are different. They're always trying to sell promising new writers. It's like working *pro bono*. Every writer—your Hemingways and your Micheners and your Stephen Kings—they all started as unknowns. Agents and publishers know this. Nothing they like better than discovering the next Elmore Leonard. It's rare, first books making money. But good writers will make everybody money in the long run."

"So maybe you can recommend someone for me, Al. Someone who'll give this book a look. I mean, if it's got some potential."

"No. I can't."

"Well, sure, if it's not—"

"You said you didn't read it."

"No."

"You should read it."

"Well, when you send it back, maybe I will."

"You missed the point," said Al.

"The point?"

"Look," he said. "I'm not quite finished with it. But this thing is absolute dynamite. It's wild. An incredible yarn. A genuine page-turner, and not that badly written. It's a fucking powder keg, Brady. Bestseller material, handled right. This guy's got a fantastic imagination."

"You mean . . . ?"

"I mean I want it. Listen, I've got to finish it, and there are a few people I want to show it to. But as far as I'm concerned, you can tell your friend there that he can expect to be rich and famous real soon."

"I'm not sure he cares about rich, and I have a strong feeling he's dead set against famous."

"I think," said Al, "that we won't be able to avoid the rich part. Preserving his anonymity can probably be done. Still, eventually I'll need to talk with him."

"I'll see what he says."

"No disrespect, Brady, but you know you're superfluous here. The agent's the one who handles all the legal stuff, and I'd prefer to deal directly with the writer." He hesitated. "Or are you interested in a piece of the action?"

"I have no interest in the action," I said. "I'm just helping out a friend here."

"Whatever," he said. "I'll get back to you in a couple weeks. Meantime, ask—what'd you say his name was? Daniel?"

"Daniel, yes."

"Tell Daniel that he and I will have some work to do. I don't want to mess with his story, but there are some loose ends and rough spots. You might mention the rich and famous part to him, too."

I called Daniel as soon as I hung up from Al Coleman. I got his answering machine at the house, so I tried the shop. A male voice I didn't recognize said, "Yo?"

"Is Daniel there?"

"Hang on."

I heard him yell, "Hey, Daniel. Phone." There was a murmur of male voices in the background, a burst of laughter.

A minute later Daniel said, "McCloud."

"It's Brady."

"Yes?"

"Daniel, I've found an agent who's agreed to handle your book. He hasn't quite finished reading it, and he wants to show it to some other people. But he loves it."

"Yes. Fine."

"His name is Al Coleman. The Coleman Agency in New York."

"Okay."

"Listen," I said. "Do you understand?"

"Aye."

"It means you've got a helluva chance of getting it published."

"I understand that."

"You don't exactly sound elated."

"It's what I expected, Brady."

I paused for a moment. "Can you talk?"

"Not really."

"You've got a gang in the shop?"

"Aye."

"And you don't want them to know about the book, right?"

"Right."

"Well, that's a damn shame, because your most appropriate reaction right now should be to jump up onto your woodstove and dance a jig."

"Hold on, will you?" he said. Then I heard him say, "Hang this up when I tell you, Vinnie."

A minute later I heard a click, and Daniel said, "Okay, Vinnie. Hang it up." Then he said, "Brady, you there?"

"I'm here."

"I'm in the office now. Noisy out there."

"And you didn't want to be overheard."

"Aye. I want to tell you something."

"Go ahead."

"I don't want to dance a jig, lad. I don't want to celebrate. This book is not an ego thing. It's just a story that I wanted to tell. Do you get it?"

"Shit, Daniel, most people—"

"Most people who write books want to be writers, see their name on the jacket of a book, be on television."

I found myself nodding. "I hear you."

"Not me."

"Okay."

"You understand?"

"Yes, Daniel."

"Well, fine."

"What about meeting with Al Coleman?"

"No."

"But if he's going to represent you—"

"He'll do it through you. And I don't want you to tell him who I am."

"Right."

"Or the publisher, or the editor, or anybody else."

"Okay."

"That's your job, Brady. To make sure nobody knows."

"That's what I'll tell Al, then."

After I hung up with Daniel, I called Coleman back. "He won't meet with you," I said.

"Not good," he said.

"He's adamant."

"I'll have to live with it, then."

"Something else you should know, Al."

"Go ahead."

"I doubt if this guy intends to write another book. I mean, it's not that he burns to be a writer. I suspect he's got this one story in him, and now he's told it."

"You trying to discourage me?"

"No. Just being straight with you."

"Normally," he said, "that would be important information. In this case, I don't care."

"It's that good, huh?"

"I told you. This story's dynamite."

Julie buzzed me in my office after lunch on a Tuesday a couple of weeks later. "It's the Coleman Literary Agency," she said.

"Hot-damn," I replied. "I got it."

I pressed the blinking button on my phone console and said, "Al?"

"This is Bonnie," came the voice in the phone. "Please hold for Mr. Coleman."

"Hey, Bonnie?" I said quickly.

"Yes?"

"I remember you."

"I remember you, too, Mr. Coyne."

"You and Al used to come to our place. I should've made the connection before."

"It was a long time ago."

"I guess I just didn't expect that you and Al Coleman . . ."

"Would end up married."

"Well, yes."

"Because I'm taller than him."

"Well—"

"And he's not as handsome as, for example, you."

"I didn't—"

"Al Coleman, Mr. Coyne, was a terrific lover."

"Yeah?"

"Yeah. Still is. Here. I'll put him on."

I heard a click, then, "Brady?"

"Hi, Al."

"Brady, I'm sending back the manuscript."

"Huh?"

"I've decided not to handle it."

"But I thought—"

"Dynamite. I know. I said that. I thought it was a fucking novel." He paused. "Listen, Brady. I shouldn't've even called you. I should just send it back with the standard rejection form. But—listen. How well do you know this guy?"

"Daniel?"

"Yes. Is he really a friend of yours?"

"Well, yes. He's a client. Most of my clients are friends."

"Known him for a long time?"

"Not really. Look. What makes the difference?"

I heard Al clear his throat. "Brady, I probably shouldn't be telling you this. But I'd feel guilty if I didn't, okay?"

"For Christ sake, Al—"

"If I were you, I'd avoid this man like the plague."

"What?"

"Just give him back his manuscript, tell him it's unpublishable, and get the hell out of there. You don't want to be mixed up with this guy. He's a very scary man. He's dangerous."

"Come on, Al. I mean, shit, it's just a book. You—"

"You should trust me on this, Brady."

"Look, if you don't want the book . . ."

I heard him sigh. "I'll return the book. You read it. Then you can judge for yourself, okay? Hey, someone'll probably publish it. Good luck to you. But not me. I don't need it. I don't need the money that bad. I'm just not gonna get involved with a guy like that."

"Jesus Christ, Al—"

"Read the book, Brady. Then you'll see what I mean."

7

I swiveled around and stared out the window onto Copley Square. Al Coleman had loved Daniel's book, wanted it, thought it had bestseller potential. Then suddenly he hated it. He didn't say it was a bad book, boring, poorly written, any of the usual things that get books rejected. Instead, he talked about Daniel. A scary, dangerous man, he called him. What kind of reason is that to reject a book?

I knew Daniel. Not well, maybe, but a helluva lot better than Al Coleman. I suppose anyone who had survived the Vietnam jungle nightmare could be seen as scary. Daniel struck me as troubled, perhaps. Depressed, edgy, maybe a little paranoid. But he wasn't scary or dangerous.

And so what if he was? Lots of scary, sick, perverted people published popular books. It made no sense.

I'd make sure to read it when I got it back. Maybe then I'd understand Al's reaction.

I went back to the library and photocopied the entire

three-page listing of literary agents from a volume called *The Writer's Handbook*. I called every one of them, told them about Daniel's book, and found four who agreed to bypass the usual narrative outline preliminary and look at the manuscript, and who said they didn't mind what they called a "simultaneous submission." As soon as the manuscript came back I would make copies of it and send it to all four of them.

I told Daniel what had happened. He accepted that news with typical stoicism. He didn't ask why Al had changed his mind, and I was relieved that I didn't have to tell him. I told him I'd try to find another agent to handle it.

Two weeks passed from the day that Al Coleman had called to reject the book. The manuscript didn't arrive.

I called the Coleman Agency. A machine answered. I tried several times over the next two or three days. I would always get the machine with Bonnie's voice informing me that I should leave my name and number and my call would be promptly returned.

I did as instructed. My call wasn't returned at all.

This irritated the hell out of me. I decided I'd call Al Coleman at home. At dinnertime. Or late at night. I can't stand being ignored.

So I once again scurried over to the library and copied all of the Albert and Allen and Alan and Alfred and Alvin Colemans out of the Manhattan phone directory. There were twenty-three of them.

After supper that evening I began calling.

On my fourteenth try I got a machine with Bonnie's voice on it. I left a message there, too. I tried again at midnight, just before I went to bed. Again the machine answered. I didn't bother leaving a message this time.

I decided Al and Bonnie had gone on vacation.

A week later they were still on vacation.

And they were still on vacation five weeks later. It was the last week in September, and Al Coleman still hadn't returned Daniel McCloud's book to me.

When the phone beside my bed began jangling, I tried to reach for it. But I found that my arm, draped over Terri Fiori's hip, had gone to sleep and refused to awaken as fast as my head did.

"Someone's at the door," Terri mumbled.

"It's the telephone, hon."

"So get the phone already."

"I can't move my arm."

Terri moaned, turned, kissed my neck, reached across me, and picked up the phone. She had to slide the entire front of her body against the front of mine when she did it. It helped to wake me up. She held the receiver to my ear. She rubbed her smooth leg against mine and nuzzled my throat.

"Cut it out," I whispered.

She bit my numb shoulder.

"Hello?" I said into the phone.

"Brady?"

"Yes. Who's this?"

"It's Cammie Russell. Brady, something's happened."

I pushed myself up so that I was half sitting in the bed. "What's the matter?"

Terri pulled away from me and frowned.

"It's Daniel," said Cammie.

"What—?"

"He's . . . he wasn't in the house. I went to the shop. He's . . . they killed him."

"What?"

"He's dead. An arrow. Brady, I'm trying to keep it together here, but I don't know if . . ."

"Call the police and sit tight, Cammie. I'm on my way."

"No."

"No?"

"I can't call them."

"You've got to."

"No. I can't. It's—"

"Because of Oakley?"

"Yes."

"You think . . . ?"

"I'm not calling them, Brady."

I mouthed the word "coffee" to Terri. With the phone wedged between my shoulder and my ear, I fumbled on the bedside table for a cigarette. Terri kissed my belly and scurried bareass into the kitchen. I got a Winston lit and said into the phone, "Okay, Cammie. I'll be there in two hours. Stay in the house and lock the door. Don't answer the phone or let anybody in until I get there. Okay?"

"Okay."

"Are you all right?"

"I'm okay. But Daniel's dead. He's the only . . ."

"I'm on my way."

When I told Terri about it, she insisted on coming with me. She said that Cammie might appreciate having a woman there. I didn't argue with her. We filled a thermos with coffee and bought some crullers on the way to the turnpike entrance. I kept the needle on eighty all the way out the pike and was grateful that the state police had set no speed traps on that Sunday morning.

I pulled up in front of Daniel's house a few minutes before nine. Terri followed me up to the front door. I banged on it and yelled, "Cammie. It's Brady."

The door opened almost instantly. I suspected she had been at a window watching for me. "Thank you," she said. "I just . . ."

I put my arms around her and held her against me. Her body was limp and loose. Her head rested against my shoulder. I patted her back. "Are you all right?"

"Yes. I don't know. I keep thinking maybe I was wrong. Can we go see him?"

"Yes." I stepped back, then remembered Terri. "Cammie, this is my friend Terri Fiori."

Cammie nodded. "Hi." They shook hands.

We went down to the shop. I opened the door and went in. The two women followed behind me.

"Be careful not to touch anything," I said to them.

Daniel was sprawled on his back near the woodstove. He looked shrunken and pale and incredibly still, lying there on the floor in a lake of his own dark blood. The feathered end of an arrow protruded at an angle from his midsection. It had sliced through his T-shirt and entered his body just above his navel, then penetrated upward under his rib cage, neatly avoiding bone along the way. About a foot of arrow was visible. Since hunting arrows are usually thirty inches long, I figured a good foot and a half had sliced its way up through Daniel's diaphragm and into his chest cavity.

He had bled vastly from the entry wound. The front of his T-shirt was drenched, and a puddle the size and general shape of a bathtub surrounded his body. Broadheads are designed to maximize bleeding, and this one had done its job. An animal shot with a hunting arrow generally dies from blood loss, except when a lucky shot happens to nick its heart.

I guessed, in Daniel's case, that his assassin had got off a lucky shot. There was no way that arrow hadn't punctured his heart.

I squatted beside him, careful not to step in the congealed blood. His eyes were open and glazed and staring upward. He was obviously dead, but I pressed my fingers under his jaw anyway, seeking a pulse. There was none.

I got up, went to the phone beside the cash register, and dialed 911. I told the cop who answered that we had a dead body and gave him the address.

After I hung up, I turned to Cammie and Terri. They were standing by the doorway watching me. Terri had her arm around Cammie's shoulders.

"They'll be here in a minute," I told them. "Let's wait outside."

The three of us sat on the front steps of Daniel's shop. I smoked a cigarette. Cammie and Terri sat close to each other. Terri still had her arm around Cammie and was holding her hand. The September sun filtered through the big maples that overhung the building. Somewhere behind us a few crows argued.

"Any thoughts?" I said to Cammie.

"Oakley," she murmured after a moment.

"Come on," I said. "So he arrested Daniel. That doesn't mean—"

"I can't think of anyone else."

"Can you remember anything Daniel ever said that might make you think someone would want to murder him? Somebody other than Oakley, I mean?"

"No."

"When do you think it happened?"

"Sometime after midnight. We were together last night until about then. We started to watch *Saturday Night Live*, but I was tired so we shut it off after the first couple of skits. Daniel walked me back to my place, kissed me goodnight, and I went right to bed. He mentioned he had a few things to clean up, that he'd be up for a while. Daniel would often go to the shop late at night. You know, to take inventory, work on his accounts, stack the shelves, look after the bait tanks. When he was working on his book, that's where he went. He didn't sleep much. He was always restless at night."

"But he didn't hint that he might be meeting somebody?"

She shook her head.

I looked hard at her. "He was running out of grass, wasn't he?"

She shrugged. "He still had some."

"But he knew he'd be needing more."

"It worried him, yes."

"Did he say anything about finding a source?"

She gazed away from me. "Not really."

"What do you mean?"

Her eyes returned to mine. "He was trying to cut back. To parcel out what he had left. He talked about having to do something. You know Daniel. He never complained. But he knew he couldn't live without his medicine. And he wouldn't buy it from a dealer."

"Nothing more specific than that?"

She shook her head. "No."

"And you didn't hear anything last night? A car, voices?"

"My studio's way out back. I was asleep."

At that moment we heard a siren's wail racing toward us. Then a police cruiser came careening into the parking area in front of the shop. Two uniformed cops emerged unhurriedly. Neither of them was Sergeant Oakley.

I stood up and went to meet them. "Brady Coyne," I said. "I made the call."

They both nodded. Neither offered his hand or his name. The younger of the two, a compact, dark-haired guy in his twenties, wandered over to where Cammie and Terri were sitting on the steps.

"What've we got?" said the other cop, a paunchy guy about fifteen years older.

"Daniel McCloud has been killed. With a hunting arrow. He's in there." I jerked my thumb backward, indicating his shop.

"McCloud, huh?" The cop shook his head. "Nice guy, McCloud. I usta buy bait from him." He looked over my shoulder toward Cammie and Terri. "The black one's his lady friend. Who's the other one?"

"She came with me."

"And you, Mr. Coyne?"

"I'm Daniel's lawyer. Cammie called me. She's the one who found his body. I drove up from Boston."

"Boston, huh? What's that, two hours on the pike?"

"I made it in an hour-forty."

"How come she didn't call us right away?"

I shrugged. "I guess she was pretty upset. Confused, you know?"

"She should've called right away."

"I know."

"She see anything?"

"She says no."

"And you?"

"I went in and looked at his body. He's dead."

"Shot with an arrow, huh?"

I nodded.

"Well," said the cop, "we'll just sit tight until the detectives get here and try not to mess up the crime scene."

At that moment I heard another siren, and a moment later an unmarked sedan pulled in beside the cruiser. It was followed shortly by an ambulance, then a state police cruiser, then another unmarked sedan.

For the next hour or so, state and local police, forensic experts, EMTs, photographers, and medical examiners swarmed around Daniel's place. Cammie, Terri, and I each had our own detective to question us. Mine was Lieutenant Dominick Fusco, a tall swarthy guy with thick, curly iron-gray hair. He told me he knew my friend Horowitz, a state cop from the Boston area.

I told Fusco that Daniel was both my client and my friend and I couldn't think of anybody—aside, possibly, from Sergeant Oakley of the Wilson Falls Police Department—who didn't like him. I said that I didn't think the bait and tackle business was likely to create murderous competition.

I also told him that Daniel used marijuana for medicine, and that his homegrown year's supply had been confiscated by the police in July, although the case against Daniel had been dismissed. Fusco said he knew all about that, and the implication was clear. They'd be checking out all the local drug sources closely.

Fusco told me that it looked as if Daniel's killer had ransacked the little office in back of the shop. He asked me if that suggested anything to me. I said robbery, obviously. He said there was still money in the cash register and it didn't look as if anything had been stolen from the shop.

If it wasn't robbery, then nothing suggested itself to me.

Otherwise, Fusco didn't tell me anything. And I didn't have much to tell him, either.

After a while the EMTs wheeled a stretcher out of the shop. A lumpy black bag was on the stretcher. It was loaded into the back of the ambulance, which then drove away. It didn't bother to sound its siren.

And, one by one, the various police cruisers and

sedans pulled away. Fusco was the last to leave. He had taken notes as we talked. I had given him both my office and home phone numbers.

He tucked his noteook into his jacket pocket. "We'll be in touch, Mr. Coyne," he said.

"Anything I can do, let me know."

"You can count on it."

He turned to go to his car. I said, "I've been thinking."

He stopped. "Yeah?"

"I don't think he was shot with a bow."

Fusco smiled. "No?"

"No. The angle of that arrow. Assuming he was standing up, to shoot him, you'd have to be lying on the floor."

"That's pretty elementary, Mr. Coyne."

I shrugged. "Guess so."

"They didn't shoot him," he said. "Somebody rammed that arrow into him."

"That's what I was thinking," I said. "He was standing there in front of him, or maybe beside him, and he grabbed that arrow with both hands and just shoved it in as hard as he could."

Fusco nodded. "Raises all kinds of questions, once you think of it that way, huh?"

"Yes," I said.

"Well," he said, "you have any further insights, or hypotheses, or questions, or anything, you be sure to let me know, okay?"

"You bet," I said.

8

We were still standing there, a few minutes after the last official vehicle had left, when a banged-up old Ford pickup chugged to a stop in the driveway.

"Oh, gee," muttered Cammie.

A vastly overweight black man climbed out the passenger side and a powerful-looking swarthy guy got out from behind the wheel. Cammie met them halfway. The three of them formed a huddle with their arms around each other's shoulders. They leaned forward so that their foreheads appeared to be touching. I could hear the low rumble of the black man's voice. It sounded as if he was praying.

After a few minutes, they straightened up. Cammie took each man by the arm and led the two of them back toward where Terri and I stood.

"Brady Coyne, Terri Fiori, this is Roscoe Pollard"—indicating the fat black man—"and Vinnie Colletti. Daniel's dear friends."

I stepped forward and shook hands with each of

them. Roscoe's eyes were large and dark and damp. "Hello, brother," he said softly in a deep bass voice.

Vinnie, who was shaped like a linebacker, said nothing when we shook. His eyes refused to meet mine.

Each of them nodded shyly at Terri.

"I called Vinnie and Roscoe right before you got here," Cammie said to me.

"You should've called sooner, sister," said Roscoe, who I took to be the spokesman for the two men. "We're only twenty minutes away. You shouldn't have been alone."

Cammie nodded. "I know. It was . . . I guess I wasn't thinking very clearly. I called Brady right away, he said he was coming, and . . ." She shrugged.

"You're Daniel's lawyer," said Roscoe to me. Up close, I saw that he was fat like a sumo wrestler. All that flesh was composed of great mounds of muscle.

"Yes," I said to him. "His lawyer."

"You got him out of jail."

I shrugged and nodded.

"Daniel talked about you. He liked you."

"I liked him, too."

He dipped his head in a kind of a bow. "Thank you for coming."

I nodded.

"We got here as fast as we could," he said to Cammie. "The, um, all the official vehicles were already here. We decided to wait till they left. No sense of confusing things."

Cammie smiled and nodded.

Roscoe turned to me. "Me and Vinnie live up the road a ways. Turner's Falls. We were with Daniel over there. We were family. We helped him build this." He waved at the shop and the house. "We hung around with him. Shooting the shit in the shop. Fishing, hunting, catching bait." He shook his head.

I understood that Roscoe and Vinnie had chosen to wait for the police to leave before they made their appearance. Their motives, I figured, were their own business.

"Let's go up to the house," said Cammie. "We'll have coffee."

The five of us went up to the house. Cammie, with her arms around the massive backs of the two big men, looked like a child between them.

We took coffee out onto the deck. Cammie sat staring dry-eyed off toward the river. It would take a while to sink in. Roscoe and Vinnie said little. Vinnie Colletti, in fact, had barely uttered a word since he arrived. Neither Terri nor I tried to disturb the somber mood. We all sat there with our own thoughts.

Sometime later we heard the sound of a motorcycle moving fast toward the house. Cammie jumped up without speaking and walked quickly around to the front.

Roscoe and Vinnie exchanged smiles. They remained on the deck.

Terri and I followed behind Cammie. As we got there, we saw a helmeted man skid a big Harley to a stop in the driveway. He leaped off his bike, took off his helmet, and held out his arms to Cammie. She ran to him and hugged herself against him. He held her for a long time. They swayed back and forth, and it was hard to tell who was comforting whom.

He was a tall, very thin man with a deeply creased face and a scraggly beard. He murmured into Cammie's ear. I noticed that Cammie was crying against his shoulder.

After several minutes the man lifted his head and noticed me and Terri. He whispered something to Cammie, who turned to look at us. Then she stepped out of his embrace, took his hand, and led him to us.

"Brady Coyne, Terri Fiori, this is Brian. Brian Sweeney."

Sweeney held out his hand to me and we shook. He dipped his head shyly and murmured, "Mr. Coyne." Then he turned to Terri and smiled. "Ma'am," he said.

"Brady is Daniel's lawyer," said Cammie. "And friend."

Sweeney nodded. "He's mentioned you," he said to me. He turned back to Cammie. "I came just as soon as I got your message. Sorry I wasn't quicker."

"Brian lives in Vermont," said Cammie. "He doesn't have a phone. You have to call the general store." She moved beside him and snaked her arm around his waist. "Brian is Daniel's best friend in the world."

"What in hell happened?" he said.

"Someone shoved a hunting arrow into his heart," I said.

"Jesus," Sweeney muttered. "They know who?"

"If they do they're not saying."

"An *arrow*?"

I nodded. "Yes. I saw it."

Up close, I could see that Sweeney was younger than I had at first thought. Early forties at the most, I guessed, about the same age as Roscoe and Vinnie. Barely twenty when he prowled the jungles of Indochina with Daniel. But already his hair was thinning and his skinny body was growing stooped and lines were etching themselves on his face. Under its ruddy sunbaked surface his skin seemed dull and sickly.

He stared solemnly at me. "This is hard to believe," he said. "I mean, *Daniel?* An *arrow?* Christ, there ain't *nobody*—" I saw his Adam's apple bob in his long throat, and then tears welled up in his eyes. "Ah, shit," he said. He turned to Cammie and pulled her against him. "Ah, damn, anyhow," he mumbled into her hair. "He was all we had," he said to her. "Both of us."

"Roscoe and Vinnie are here," Cammie told him.

"Good," said Sweeney.

The four of us went back to the house. Sweeney exchanged complicated ritualistic handshakes with Roscoe and Vinnie and then gave each of them a bear hug. The three of them wandered down to the end of the deck, where they stood close together, murmuring.

After a few minutes they came back. Tears glittered in Roscoe's eyes.

"You guys want sandwiches?" said Cammie.

"Good idea," said Sweeney.

Cammie and Terri went inside. I sat down with the other three men and lit a cigarette. Sweeney took a Sucrets box from his shirt pocket, flipped its lid, and removed a prerolled cigarette. He held the box to Roscoe and Vinnie. They both shook their heads.

Sweeney lit up, sucked in, and held it in his lungs.

Then he sighed. "We were all there together," he said to me, jerking his head at the other two men.

"Vietnam?"

He nodded.

"All of you stayed close."

They all nodded.

"It was Daniel," said Roscoe softly. "He kept us together. That's why we all ended up around here. To stick by Daniel."

"So who'd want to kill him?" I said.

The three of them shrugged.

"What about you?" said Sweeney to me. "Do you have any thoughts?"

"You mean, who killed Daniel?"

He nodded.

"Well, he was worried that he was running out of his medicine."

"Yeah," said Sweeney. "Me, too. Daniel kept both of us supplied."

"You—?"

He nodded. "I got Oranged, too. We talked about it after they ripped up his garden. But Daniel wouldn't deal with any supplier. I might," he added with a sly grin, "but not Daniel."

"The only other thing I can think of, then," I said, "is this local cop, this Sergeant Oakley, the one who arrested Daniel. Cammie suspects him, I think. But that seems pretty farfetched to me."

Sweeney shrugged. "Daniel was a lovable old bastard," he said.

I flashed back on Al Coleman's words. Coleman had called Daniel crazy and dangerous. "You sure of that?" I said.

The three of them all frowned at me. "What do you mean?" said Roscoe.

"Somebody didn't love him. Somebody killed him."

He shrugged. "Someone who didn't know him, then."

"A burglar, maybe."

"Nah," said Sweeney quickly. "No burglar would get the drop on him like that. Daniel was too quick and too careful for any burglar. Was anything stolen?"

"I don't think so. The office behind his shop was ransacked. But apparently nothing was taken."

Sweeney stared across the meadow. "I can do some checking around," he said. He glanced at Roscoe and Vinnie. "We all can."

"What are you thinking?"

He shrugged. "A man leads a team into the jungle . . ."

"You should share your thoughts with the police," I said. "You all should."

Sweeney turned to me. "I haven't got any thoughts," he said. "But I'm gonna check around anyway."

9

Lieutenant Fusco called me from Springfield a few days later. But I had no further insights for him. I realized that I hadn't known Daniel McCloud that well. I had represented him when he was arrested, and I had tried to find an agent for his book.

He was more than a client. Most of my clients are. I considered him a friend. But he was also a private man. He hadn't shared his demons with me, though I suspected that any man who had lived through the things he had lived through must be haunted. Cammie, more candidly than Daniel, had suggested as much.

Fusco had no insights, either, or at least none he chose to share with me. He did tell me that they had made no arrests, discovered no motive, identified no suspects. Cammie inventoried the shop for them, and they concluded that there had been no robbery. The office in the back had been messed up, but nothing appeared to be missing.

The medical examiner, Fusco told me, determined that Daniel had died almost instantly when the broadhead sliced through his heart. There was no evidence, either at the crime scene or on Daniel's body, of a struggle between him and his assailant. They had found no useful fingerprints or footprints or tire tracks, no stray human hairs or bits of skin, no scraps of fabric or lost buttons, no cigar ashes or cigarette butts. No witnesses. Nothing.

Terri and I took turns talking with Cammie on the phone each day during the week following Daniel's death. Roscoe Pollard and Vinnie Colletti, she told us, had left shortly after we did the day Daniel was killed. Brian Sweeney stayed a little longer, but then he, too, left. Daniel's army buddies, she said, were a lot like Daniel. They didn't like to stray far from home. But Sweeney, especially, was a comfort, and he called her every day, too, the way Terri and I did.

The state police had interrogated her repeatedly. She had to tell them her entire life story, and Daniel's, too, or what she knew of it. She gave them the names of everybody she could think of who knew Daniel—Roscoe Pollard and Vinnie Colletti and Brian Sweeney and his other "brothers" from Vietnam and the local guys who liked to hang around at the bait and tackle shop. She told me she thought they had arranged for a Vermont state police detective to talk with Sweeney, who was Daniel's best friend and had known him longer and better than anybody, including herself.

She had to tell them about how Daniel had rescued her from her Springfield pimp. That wasn't easy, she said.

She didn't like the way the cops glanced at each other out of the corners of their eyes or the exaggerated way they called her "Ma'am." But they had to know about Boomer.

She was okay, she told us. She said she guessed it still hadn't really hit her yet.

I figured the police regarded Cammie Russell as a suspect.

The following Saturday, just a week after the murder, Terri and I spent the day with Cammie. The three of us walked through the woods and along the river that Daniel had loved. Cammie and Terri seemed to like each other, which made sense to me, since I liked both of them. They whispered between themselves, and a couple of times Cammie laughed. Later, I grilled steaks for the three of us while Cammie and Terri tossed a big salad, and we ate out on the deck while Daniel's favorite Jimmy Reed tape played through the sliding screens. We had some wine and watched the sun sink over the river. Darkness settled into the woods and the night creatures came out. We put our heads back and looked at the stars. We switched to coffee.

"As soon as they release his body," said Cammie, "I'm going to give a party. I hope you both will come."

"Of course," I said.

"And then," she said to me, "I'll probably need to talk with a lawyer."

"Yes. I'll help all I can."

She reached over and squeezed my arm. "I know. You already have."

It was midnight. Terri yawned. We took the coffee mugs inside. "Thanks a lot for coming," said Cammie.

"We can stay with you," I said.

"I'm fine."

"Are you sure?"

She nodded.

I arched my eyebrows doubtfully.

She reached behind her back, then showed me the small automatic handgun that had materialized in her hand.

"Ah," I said. "You're armed."

"Daniel insisted."

"When?"

"Right from the beginning. I was afraid of Boomer coming for me. Daniel kept saying I shouldn't worry, but I wasn't very stable then. So he got this for me and showed me how to use it. I've never seen Boomer." She shrugged. "But I've just kept it."

"I thought Daniel hated guns."

"He didn't hate them. He just never felt he needed one. He thought I did."

"Do you have a license for it?"

Cammie shook her head. "Daniel said it was none of anybody's business. Anyway, he said it wouldn't be such a good idea. I do have a—I've been arrested. You have to get permits from the local police, you know."

"Oakley?" I said.

She smiled. "You know how he felt about Oakley."

"You could get in a lot of trouble, lugging that around."

"I don't lug it around. I just keep it on me when I'm around here alone, that's all. When Daniel was here, I kept it beside my bed. I feel better with it. For now. For a while."

She tucked her little weapon back into the holster at the small of her back.

Terri and I took the back roads home, through South Hadley, the self-proclaimed asparagus capital of the world, through Granby and Belchertown and Pelham and New Salem, heading north parallel to the Quabbin Reservoir, through the dark rural parts of Massachusetts. On Route 2 a few trucks whanged past us. Their backdrafts tugged at my steering wheel. Terri and I didn't talk much. I found some jazz on a Worcester radio station. They were playing a Miles Davis album. His trumpet had never sounded more blue.

"You've been awfully good to Cammie," I said to Terri.

"She's hurting a lot more than she shows."

"Does she talk to you about it?"

"Not really. She talks about Daniel. He was more like a father to her than . . ."

"I guess he saved her life."

"That's how Cammie sees it. He *was* her life. It's like she really doesn't have one now. But she's strong. I think she'll be okay."

I reached across the front seat and squeezed Terri's leg. "Well, you've obviously been good to her."

She laid her hand atop mine. "My nurse's training," she said.

As we approached the Acton turnoff, Terri said, "Brady, I think I want to sleep in my own bed tonight."

"Sure. Okay."

"Alone, I mean."

I shrugged.

"I'm sorry."

"No problem," I lied.

"I want to get Melissa first thing in the morning."

"I thought your mother had her for the weekend."

"It's what I want to do, okay?"

There was an edge to her voice that I had never heard before.

She kissed me hard and long at the door to her building, and I said, "Sure you don't want me to stay?"

"Not tonight."

I shrugged. "Okay."

"Do you understand?"

"No."

She put her arms around my neck and her cheek on my shoulder. "It's complicated."

"Try me."

"I really do want to get Melissa."

"Sure, but—"

"Okay. I want to be alone."

"You mean, you want to be apart from me."

"Yes."

"Okay. Fine."

"Try to understand, Brady. Cammie and I did a lot of talking. It's been a . . . an unsettling day."

"No problem."

"You don't understand, do you?"

"It doesn't matter."

She tipped her head back and looked into my face. "I'm sorry," she said. "I wish . . ."

"Don't worry about it," I said.

She tried to smile. It wasn't convincing.

She kissed me and pressed against me. I held her tight. After a long time she gently pulled away. "Tonight," she whispered, "I need to be alone. Just tonight. Okay?"

"You got it," I said.

She hugged me quickly, then fumbled in her purse for her keys. "Call me?"

"I will."

"Good night, Brady."

"'Night, Terri."

I walked back to the parking lot. When I got to my car, I turned to wave to Terri. But she had already gone inside.

10

I called Terri on Tuesday. "How's the weekend look?" I said.

"Not that good. I—"

"Don't give me an excuse, hon. You don't have to."

She hesitated. "I'm sorry. You're right. I was going to tell you I was all tied up with Melissa. It's true, but it's not the point. I've been all tied up with Melissa plenty of times and you've been a part of it. I don't want to get into lying or making up excuses with you, Brady."

"You don't have to. I'm a big boy."

"My feelings for you haven't changed."

"But?"

"But . . . my feelings are making me nervous. I need space."

"I guess," I said, "true love is when both people feel the need for the same amount of space at the same time."

"I always thought it was when you stopped feeling that you needed space."

"No," I said. "Everybody needs space."

I ended up spending the first day of my weekend space with my friend Doc Adams. We drank beer and played chess in his backyard in Concord, and toward the middle of the afternoon Doc mentioned a local pond that, he had heard, the state stocked with trout every September. Nobody seemed to fish there, Doc told me. Doc wasn't much for fly-fishing himself. He thought it a pretty yuppified sport, actually. He tried it a few times, and on one especially windy afternoon on the Deerfield River he drove a hook beyond the barb into his earlobe. I yanked it out for him—Doc never uttered a peep—and that was enough fly-fishing for him. But he loved to eat fresh-caught trout and he wondered if a man who claimed to be a good fly-fisherman might be able to harvest a meal from this secret pond of his.

Doc even volunteered to paddle the canoe and clean the fish afterward as well, should I get lucky.

The surface of the pond was littered with crimson and yellow maple leaves, which skittered around like toy sailboats ahead of a light puffy breeze. We saw lots of migrating birds—ducks in the coves and warblers in the pondside bushes—and I managed to catch a dozen or so fat ten-inch brook trout on gaudy little wet flies. We kept six and brought them back to Doc's house on Old Stone Mill Road. Doc sautéed them in butter with tarragon and shallots while his wife, Mary, and I drank wine and kibitzed. Mary asked about Terri. I told her that Terri was tied up with her daughter for the weekend. Mary cocked her head and looked at me sideways. I shrugged. She didn't pursue it.

The trout were delicious. Doc asserted that we could've caught twice as many using spinning gear. We argued our respective definitions of sport.

Mary said she knew a young sculptress, recently divorced. I told her I didn't think I was interested. She smiled and said she thought as much, but figured she should mention it.

Sunday morning I called the house in Wellesley. I wanted to say hello to Joey, my younger son. The answering machine took it. Gloria asked me to leave my name and number and the time of my call. I declined her invitation.

I tried Billy, my other son, at his dorm room at UMass. No answer.

So much for family ties.

I spent the afternoon rummaging distractedly through the weekend paperwork that Julie had stuffed into my briefcase. That evening around suppertime Cammie called. "Can you come to a party next Saturday afternoon?" she said.

"Yes. Wouldn't miss it."

"Dress casual."

"Gladly."

"They're releasing Daniel's body on Tuesday."

"Do they have any new evidence?"

"If they do, they're not sharing it with me."

"I'll give Lieutenant Fusco a call," I said, "see what he knows. I'll be there Saturday."

"Please bring Terri."

"I'll try."

After a hesitation, she said, "Is something the matter?"

"I don't know. A boy-girl thing, I guess."

She chuckled. "Tell her I'll be very sad if she doesn't come."

"I'll tell her exactly that."

And I did. I said, "Cammie will be very sad if you don't come."

"You don't need to do that, Brady," said Terri. "Of course I'll go with you. I hope *you'd* be sad if I didn't go."

"That's the truth. I missed you this weekend."

"Wow," she said softly.

"Wow?"

"That's about the most vulnerable thing you've ever said to me."

"I don't always say what I'm thinking."

"Maybe you should try it more often."

I pondered that bit of advice after I hung up with her. I concluded that, on the whole, it was dangerous advice.

I called State Police Lieutenant Dominick Fusco on Monday morning. He was unavailable. I requested he return my call. He didn't. I tried again Tuesday, and then on Wednesday. Finally, on Thursday afternoon, Julie buzzed me and said that Lieutenant Fusco was on the line.

I pressed the blinking button on my console and said, "Coyne."

"Fusco," he said. "What can you do for me?"

"I was just wondering how the Daniel McCloud investigation is going."

"That's what I figured. That's why I didn't call you right back."

"Well . . ."

"You haven't got anything for me, right?"

"Right."

"Mr. Coyne," said Fusco, "we don't normally feel obligated to share the progress of our investigations with citizens. If we did that, we'd have no time for investigating."

"Yeah, but—"

"Daniel McCloud's murder is not the only case on my agenda just now, Mr. Coyne. Here's how it works, okay? You got something for me, you make sure I know it. That's your duty as a citizen, lawyer or no lawyer. If I come up with something, I'll probably pursue the hell out of it. But it's possible I might not have the time or the inclination to share it with you. Get it?"

"This conversation we're having here is what you call effective public relations," I said. "Right?"

"My job," said Fusco, "ain't relating to the public. My job is arresting them when they break the law."

"Be nice, then, if you'd do your job."

I think Fusco and I hung up on each other simultaneously. Goes to show what happens when you say what you're thinking.

Terri and I had to park about a quarter of a mile from Daniel's house on Saturday afternoon. Daniel's friends had turned out in force. I hadn't realized he had that many friends. The roadside was lined with parked vehicles. Battered old pickups, mainly, with a few battered old sedans, most of them Fords and Chevvies. My BMW was one of the few unbattered vehicles in the bunch.

Terri and I walked to the house holding hands. We

wore jeans and flannel shirts and windbreakers and sneak-
ers. Twins. Terri looked especially terrific in jeans. The way
she squeezed my hand and bumped shoulders with me as
we walked was terrific, too. It occurred to me that maybe
she had satisfied her need for space for a while.

We weaved our way among the guests as we made our
way toward the back of the house. I guessed there were
close to a hundred people milling around Daniel's property
holding plastic glasses or beer cans. I didn't recognize anybody, but several of them said, "Hey, how ya doin?" to me
and Terri anyway. Rural good-neighborliness.

The bar was set up on the deck behind the house.
That's where we found Cammie. When she saw us she
smiled and came over. Brian Sweeney was with her. His
hand was wrapped around a beer can, and the stub of a
dead cigar was wedged into the corner of his mouth.
Cammie had her arm tucked through his.

She exchanged quick kisses with Terri and gave me a
big hug. Sweeney shook my hand and gave Terri a little
courtly bow.

"Thanks for coming, you guys," said Cammie.

"Wouldn't have missed it," I said.

A man about Sweeney's age grabbed his arm.
Sweeney whirled around, yelled, "Holy shit," and
embraced him. They wandered away, their arms across
each other's shoulders.

Cammie watched them for a moment, then turned
back to us. She smiled. "Nothing tighter than army buddies," she said. She cocked her head at me. "Maybe later we
can do some business?"

I nodded. "Of course."

Cammie turned to Terri, bent, and whispered something to her. Terri nodded. "Let me borrow her for a minute, okay?" said Cammie to me.

I shrugged. "Sure."

The two of them wandered away. Cammie had her hand on Terri's shoulder. I had the feeling they were discussing me.

So I found myself standing there on the deck. I was surrounded by people, but I was alone. I spotted Roscoe Pollard and Vinnie Colletti. Roscoe noticed me and waved. I waved back. I found several big washtubs full of ice and Budweiser. I went over and fished out two cans. I weaved through the people toward Cammie and Terri. The two women were leaning their elbows on the deck railing, staring off toward the river and talking softly, their heads close together. I pressed the cold beer can against Terri's neck. "Hey!" she squealed. She spun around and glared at me. I held up the Bud. "Oh," she said. "Thanks."

She took the can and turned back to her conversation with Cammie.

I shrugged and wandered off the deck and out into the yard. I started to head toward the knot of people that included Roscoe and Vinnie, then changed my mind. I felt like an outsider.

So I stood there. I sipped from my beer and lit a cigarette.

A hand squeezed my elbow. "You get the cold shoulder, there, Mr. Coyne?"

It was Sweeney. I smiled. "From the ladies?" I nodded. "Looks like it. And it's Brady, okay?"

"Yeah," he said. "Okay."

We found ourselves sauntering away from the crowd in the yard, headed more or less in the direction of the river. Sweeney, I guessed, like Daniel, was not comfortable in crowds.

"Listen," said Sweeney as we walked. "Daniel told me about how you kept him out of jail that time. It woulda killed him, you know?"

"I didn't really do much, truthfully," I said. "They dropped the charges before I could do anything."

"Well, he sure appreciated it."

He stopped walking to light a wooden match with his thumbnail. He ignited his cigar butt. "Hard to believe," he puffed.

"Daniel?"

He exhaled and nodded.

"That he's dead, you mean."

He shrugged. "Not so much that. I guess I never find death hard to believe anymore. How it happened, I mean."

"An ugly way to go."

He turned to face me. "There are uglier ways, Brady. Believe me. What I hear, that was pretty quick. What I mean is somebody getting the drop on him like that. I never saw Daniel with his defenses down."

"It's been a long time since you guys were in the jungle," I said.

"Don't matter. You never lose it." He removed the cigar from his mouth and took a long draft from his beer can. "You heard anything?"

I shook my head.

"No suspects, no evidence?"

"No," I said. "I talked to the state cop in charge a couple days ago. Lieutenant Fusco. Not very forthcoming. Doesn't seem to me they're getting anywhere. They questioned you, didn't they?"

"Me?" he said. "Yeah. State cops dropped by. Vermont cops. I'm living up there in the sticks. Kinda like Daniel. Little place in the woods. Catch some fish, shoot some deer." He smiled. "You don't get the jungle out of your system, you know? Anyways, they asked me about who might want to kill him. How the hell would I know?"

"You said you'd check around with the men from your team," I said.

He nodded. "I am. Most of 'em are here." He shook his head. "Hard to figure, though. I mean, somebody in command, sure, there'll be times when you want to kill the guy, if you know what I mean. But that's just the stress of it. Daniel brought us through."

"What about Roscoe and Vinnie?"

Sweeney turned his head and spat a flake of tobacco onto the ground. "Yeah," he said, "they were with us. Damn good soldiers. Good men, Roscoe and Vinnie."

"They're not . . . sick?"

"The Orange? Nope. They were the lucky ones."

"And they were close to Daniel, huh?"

"We all were close with each other. Daniel was our glue."

"He was a pretty lovable guy, from what I could see," I said.

Sweeney stopped and leaned back against the trunk of an oak tree. "Lovable," he repeated. He smiled. Sadly, I thought. "Well, he was, yes. But Daniel could fool you. You meet Daniel, you think he's this gentle teddy bear. Which he was. But in the jungle he was like some other kind of animal. I mean, a fucking predator, you know? He was completely comfortable, tuned in to every sound, every smell. He could tell you whether it was a monkey or a VC just by the sound of something moving a bush. And he could kill like no man I ever knew."

I nodded. "I guess that's how you survived."

"Were you over there, Brady?"

I shook my head.

He grinned. "Probably marching around in the streets, huh?"

I shrugged. "I did some of that, yes."

"I never hated Jane Fonda, myself," said Sweeney. "Figured most of you people just wanted us home. We wanted the same damn thing."

"That's how I felt about it."

"Old Daniel," said Sweeney, "he could be an animal in the jungle. But he wasn't an animal. He was a man." Sweeney chuckled softly. "The old Snake Eater."

"Snake Eater? Daniel?"

He nodded. "It was a term of honor. Actually, it's kind of a general name that's sometimes used for Special Forces guys. The Snake Eaters. Like Green Berets, except we all thought that was dumb. We never called ourselves Green Berets. But Daniel, that sonofabitch actually ate snakes. They taught us how to survive in the jungle, see? How to kill a snake and skin it and eat it raw. But Daniel, he already knew that. He did it when he was a kid. He'd eat any damn thing. Grubs and ants and leeches. I saw him do it. He kept tryin' to get us to do it, too. Ants I got so I could swallow. Never could get a leech down, though. No problem for Daniel. See, we were all *taught* how to eat all this stuff, but Daniel actually *did* it. He used to say, compared to the rest of it, raw snake was a 'farkin' delicacy.'"

I grinned. Sweeney had Daniel's blend of Scottish burr and Georgia farmboy down pat.

"So, anyway," he continued after a moment, "that's how come we called him Snake Eater. It's like, there are lots of godfathers. But only one you actually call Godfather. Listen, you want another beer?"

"After this conversation, I could use something."

Sweeney grinned. "Didn't mean to freak you out, there, Brady. I just—shit, I miss Daniel, that's all. Helps, talking about him."

I nodded.

"Hang on. I'll be right back."

He headed back to the house. I shaded my eyes and tried to spot Terri. I didn't see her.

Sweeney was back in a few minutes. He handed me a beer.

"Thanks," I said.

"We had to go through places where they had defoliated," he said. "We didn't know there was a problem."

"Agent Orange," I said.

He nodded. "Most of us got it. I guess Pollard and Colletti were about the only ones who didn't."

"How'd they manage to escape it?"

Sweeney shrugged. "Just lucky, I guess. Galinski died

of it. His widow got a little settlement from Uncle. Me and Daniel, we tried to get some help. Daniel's friend there . . ."

"Charlie McDevitt."

"Yeah. Charlie. He tried to help us."

"Charlie's a friend of mine. That's how I met Daniel."

"I know. When he was in jail. Anyway, Charlie tried to help us, but we got the runaround."

"Does smoking marijuana help you?" I said.

He cocked his head at me, then smiled. "Yeah. It's the only thing that helps. Daniel kept me supplied. Don't know what the fuck I'm gonna do now. Try growing my own, I guess."

A woman bumped up against Sweeney and grabbed onto his arm. "Hey, Bri'," she slurred. "How they hangin'?"

He looked at her, then smiled. He put his arm across her shoulders. "How you makin' out, Ronnie?"

"Jus' pissa."

She was probably in her forties. She was fat and graying, but she had youthful skin.

She was very drunk.

Sweened nudged her to look at me. "Ronnie Galinski," he said, "this is Brady Coyne. Daniel's lawyer."

She looked at me without interest, then turned back to Sweeney. "Don't know why the fuck I'm here," she said. "Wouldn'ta come, but Neddie woulda wanted me to. Neddie loved the bas'ard. Sumbitch got Neddie killed."

"It wasn't Daniel's fault," said Sweeney gently.

"That shit jus' ate him up, Bri'," she said. "His legs swole up and his skin fell off and his brain caught fire."

Sweeney put his arm around her. "I know, hon," he said softly. "I remember."

Sweeney glanced at me, then gently steered Ronnie Galinski away. He had his arm across her shoulders, and he was bending to her, talking to her.

Galinski. That, I recalled, was the name of the soldier who had died of Agent Orange poisoning. His widow was not, apparently, a Daniel McCloud fan.

I felt something soft brush the back of my neck. I turned around. Terri said, "Hi."

I touched her hair. "Having fun?"

"Weirdest wake I've every been to. Quite an assortment, huh?"

"Daniel's friends."

"One guy got my ear," she said. "One of Daniel's men. I wouldn't say he was exactly a friend. Tall, skinny man named Shaw. He was talking about how they all had to go through this defoliated part of the jungle, and they ended up with skin problems. It sounded as if he was blaming Daniel."

"I've been talking to Brian Sweeney. He seems to credit Daniel for getting them out of there alive."

Terri nodded. "Yeah, well this Shaw, he mainly blames Daniel for getting them in there in the first place."

A motive for murder, I thought. I did not share my thought with Terri.

We stood there together quietly for a while, watching the people and sipping our beers. It was not an uncomfortable silence between us. After a while, I said, "How's Cammie doing?"

"Good, I'd say. She seems to know everybody."

At that moment I became aware of a noise. It was a low, rising wail, and it came from the edge of the river at the far end of Daniel's property, and it took me a moment to identify it.

A bagpipe.

Gradually the hum of a hundred voices died and the wail of the pipes rose and moved into a long slow version of "Amazing Grace."

I felt a tightening in my throat and a burning in my eyes.

Bagpipes always do that to me.

Without speaking, Terri and I began to walk arm-in-arm toward the source of the music. I was aware that everybody else was following the music also, a silent mass of people moving toward the river as if hypnotized by those pipes.

The piper stood on the low bluff overlooking the Connecticut River. He was dressed in tartans and kilt. He was a big, rawboned guy, red-haired and red-faced. The crowd gathered at the bluff, a little aside from the piper. I glanced around. Nobody was smiling, nobody was talking.

He segued into "The Skye Boat Song." I heard Terri whispering beside me. "Speed bonny boat like a bird on the wing . . ."

The crowd moved and parted and Cammie and Brian Sweeney appeared, walking slowly. I noticed that they were barefoot. Sweeney's arm was around Cammie's waist. She carried a blue ceramic urn in both of her hands.

Daniel.

Behind the two of them strode seven other men, also barefoot, including Roscoe Pollard and Vinnie Colletti.

"That's Shaw," whispered Terri. "The bald one."

He was the last of the seven. The others shuffled along with their heads down. Shaw's head was up, and he appeared to be marching.

I looked around the crowd for Ronnie Galinski, but I didn't spot her. I guessed she might have passed out somewhere.

Cammie and Sweeney and the other seven filed down over the bluff to the river. The rest of us closed in behind them at the edge of the water.

The piper continued to play.

Cammie and Sweeney waded knee-deep into the water. The other seven gathered in a semicircle around them. They made cups of their hands as if they were at the altar rail receiving communion. Cammie moved from one to the other, pouring in a portion of Daniel's ashes.

The pipes rose, wailed, stopped.

It was very still there beside the river.

Sweeney held his cupped hands high in front of his face. The others imitated him. "So long, old Snake Eater," he said. I thought I could see tears glitter in his eyes.

They all let Daniel dribble through their fingers into the river.

The piper played "Danny Boy."

Cammie waded out of the river. Daniel's team followed behind her.

We all fell in behind them and moved slowly back to the yard behind Daniel's house. No one spoke.

The piper, still back on the bluff by the river, played "Going Home," the Dvorak tune. Terri wrapped her arms around my waist and cried against my chest. I rested my cheek on top of her head. I could have cried, too.

Bagpipes do that to me.

11

The guests began to shake hands and exchange hugs. The party was over. Terri and I were still standing there when Cammie came up behind me and grabbed my hand.

"Can I talk to you for a minute?" she said.

I turned to her. Her eyes were blazing. "What's the matter?"

"It's that shithead Oakley. Come see."

She led me down the driveway to the road where all the cars and pickups were parked. Every one of them had a white rectangle tucked under the windshield wiper.

I went to the nearest car, removed the ticket, and looked at it. Fifteen bucks for parking in a restricted zone. Sergeant Richard Oakley had signed it. I looked at Cammie and shrugged.

"What can we do?" she said.

"If it's illegal to park on this road, nothing."

"It's harassment," she said. "It's . . . it's perverted."

"Well," I said, scratching my head, "we could sure

make it awkward for our friend Oakley if everybody exercised his right to appeal the ticket at a clerk magistrate's hearing."

"We can't expect these people to do that. They have to work. Some of them have driven a long way to be here."

I nodded. "Not much we can do, then. I've got a feeling that complaining to the police won't do much good."

"Yeah," she said. "That's probably just what Oakley wants. I don't know what his problem is, but the hell with him. I'll pay them myself. I don't want all these people leaving with a bad taste in their mouth. Let's collect them."

Cammie and I went up and down the street, removing all the tickets. There were fifty-three of them. Oakley had made out half of them. A cop named Wentzel did the other half. It would cost Cammie over $750 to pay them all.

We went back to the house. "Don't tell anybody," she said.

"Okay."

The shadows lengthened and a chill crept into the air. The people began to drift to their cars. Cammie and Brian Sweeney stood at the edge of the driveway, shaking hands and thanking everybody for coming. Terri and I fell in line.

When we got to Cammie, she said to me, "Would you guys mind waiting? I'd like to talk to you for a minute."

"Sure. Okay."

Terri and I went back to the deck. I fished around the bottom of one of the washtubs, up to my elbow in half-melted ice, and found two cans of Budweiser. I gave one to Terri. We sat in deck chairs with our feet up on the railing and stared off toward Daniel's river.

"He's probably in Holyoke by now," I said.

She nodded.

"He'll cross the line into Connecticut by dawn."

"Brady . . ." Terri reached over and held on to my hand.

"He should reach the ocean sometime on Monday."

"That bagpiper," she said.

I nodded and sipped my beer.

After that we didn't talk. We continued to hold hands.

After a while Cammie came back and sat down beside us. She sighed deeply. "What'd you think?" she said.

"It was memorable," I said. "Perfect. Was the piper your idea?"

"Brian's," she said. "Having the rest of Daniel's team do the ashes was his idea, too. I think Daniel would've liked it."

"Me, too," I said. "Did Roscoe and Vinnie and Brian all leave?"

She nodded. "They're not very sociable. All of those guys are like that. They're just different from other people."

"I wanted to ask them something," I said.

"What?"

I hesitated. Then I said, "I guess a lot of the men got Agent Orange poisoning over there. The way Daniel did."

Cammie nodded. "Brian did. One man died of it. There were others."

"Well, it occurred to me . . ."

"You think they blame Daniel?"

"That Shaw does," said Terri.

Cammie narrowed her eyes and peered at me. "So you think . . ."

I shrugged. "There was a woman here who seemed to hate Daniel. Her husband died from the Agent Orange. Galinski."

"She was pretty drunk," said Cammie.

"I'm just trying to figure out who'd want to kill him."

Cammie nodded. "Me, too. But his army buddies? After all they went through together?"

I nodded. "I know."

We stared into the darkness for a while. I thought of all the Vietnam vets I knew. Several of them had tried to tell me about the horror they carried around in their heads. I knew that those of us who hadn't been here could never understand.

"Look," said Cammie after several minutes. "I hate to impose on you . . ."

"No problem," I said. "If you can put your hands on Daniel's papers, I'll try to sort it out for you."

"I don't exactly know what he had," she said. "Or even where he kept it. I guess we should check his office."

"At the shop?"

She nodded.

The three of us walked around the house to the shop. Cammie unlocked the door and we stepped inside. I found the light switch. It looked exactly as it had the morning we found Daniel's body there, minus the body. The large oval bloodstain was still there, black and dull. The blurry outline of a man's body was visible in the middle of it.

I heard Terri exhale quickly.

"I guess I should get in here and clean up sometime," said Cammie. "But I just . . ."

Terri put her arm around Cammie's shoulder.

We stepped gingerly around the bloodstain to the door that led to Daniel's office. It stood ajar. I pushed it open.

It was a small square room, ten by ten, no bigger. One small window. There was a desk and a file cabinet and a swivel chair. An old Underwood typewriter sat on the desk. The drawers of the desk and the cabinet hung open. Papers were scattered over the floor. It had been torn apart, all right, just as the police had said.

"Let's see what we've got," I said.

The three of us got down on our knees and gathered the papers together. They were all business records—bills, accounts, inventories, catalogs, tax records. I sorted through them and made a pile of the stuff that I might need to probate Daniel's estate.

"Is there anything missing?" I said to Cammie after we finished.

She shrugged. "I couldn't tell you. I never came in here. I didn't know anything about his business. Just that I assumed he lost money at it. This," she said, waving her hand around the little room, "was his little sanctuary. It's where he came when he was writing his book."

"He never showed it to you, huh?"

"He was very secretive about that book. He worked on it for, I don't know, three or four years. He'd sneak down here and wouldn't tell me why for the longest time. I'd tell him, I'd say, 'You meeting some girl or something?' And he'd give me that old smile and say, 'Nay, lass. No girl.' But he wouldn't say what it was. Daniel was a secretive man anyway, but I kept bugging him, and finally he admitted he was trying to write a book. I asked him what it was about. He told me not to ask. He made it clear. It was none of my business. So I didn't ask. I just knew that it was important to him and he didn't want anybody to know about it. I think it would be neat if Daniel's book got published."

I nodded. I realized that Daniel's murder had driven thoughts of his book from my mind. "I'll check with Al Coleman again, see what the holdup is. He said he was sending it right back, and that was over a month ago. There are plenty of other agents. But meanwhile, there's got to be insurance records, a will, deeds, things like that that I'll need. None of that stuff's here."

Cammie snapped her fingers. "He kept a strongbox in his bedroom closet. That's probably what you want."

We locked up the shop and went back to the house. A couple of minutes later Cammie placed a cheap metal box on the kitchen table. It wasn't locked. Inside I found several manila envelopes. Daniel had carefully labeled each of them with a black felt-tip pen. "Deed." "Will." "Automobile." "Medical." "Business." "Tax." "Insurance."

None, I noticed, was labeled "Book."

I decided to take the whole box with me. I could look through all of it later.

Then Cammie switched on the floodlights that lit up the yard, and Terri and I helped her fill plastic trash bags with beer cans and plastic glasses. There were hundreds of them — in the house, on the deck, in the gardens, all over the lawn, under the shrubbery. I told Terri that Daniel's yard after the party was our world in microcosm. She told me I was unnecessarily cynical. I said I didn't think so.

Cammie insisted that Terri and I stay for supper. We

made ham-and-Swiss-cheese-and-tomato sandwiches on whole wheat and washed them down with more beer. We had coffee on the deck.

"What are you going to do?" Terri said to Cammie as we studied the night sky.

"I don't know. Nothing for a while. Paint."

"Going to stay here?"

"For now." She shrugged.

"Will you be okay?"

She smiled. "I've got my friends," she said.

Terri asked me to spend the night with her in Acton. I accepted. She slept pressed tight against my back with her arm draped over my hip, and I lay awake for a long time with her soft breath on the back of my neck, and I knew that just then neither of us was feeling any need for space.

I also knew that that would change. It always did.

Sunday evening I emptied the manila envelopes from Daniel's strongbox onto my kitchen table and began to sort through their contents. He had everything well organized. It would be easy.

He had bequeathed the house and the studio to Cammie. The shop and its contents went jointly to Brian Sweeney, Roscoe Pollard, and Vinnie Colletti.

The last envelope I opened was the one labeled "Insurance." It contained policies on his car and his buildings, plus a modest army policy on his life. The beneficiary was Cammie.

Inside the big insurance envelope was a smaller envelope. I opened it and spilled its contents onto the table.

Photographs. Six of them. Plus two index cards.

The photos were five-by-seven black-and-white head-and-shoulder shots. Six men. On the back of each was printed a name and address. The printing did not match Daniel's.

Each of the two index cards had a name and address printed on it in Daniel's hand.

I looked at the photographs. All of them were creased and smudged and dog-eared, as if somebody had carried them around in his hip pocket for a while. I recognized none of the faces. None of the names meant anything to me.

Friends of Daniel? Distant cousins? War buddies? Agent Orange victims? Debtors or creditors?

Enemies?

I couldn't recall seeing any of the faces at Daniel's funeral party. The photos showed six adult white males, all in some stage of middle age. None was particularly distinctive.

I read the addresses. The two on the index cards were in western Massachusetts, as were two on the backs of photos. Two were in Rhode Island, one in New Hampshire, and one in New York.

I sat there at my table, puffing a cigarette and gazing out onto the dark harbor.

On Monday I called Cammie and read the eight names and addresses to her. None of them was familiar to her. None of them was anybody who had been invited to the party. As far as she could recall, Daniel had never mentioned any of them to her.

"Well," I said, "they were somebody to Daniel. They were in with his insurance papers."

"Insurance?"

"Which may or may not mean a damn thing."

"What are you going to do?"

"I don't know. Talk to these people, I guess."

"You think . . . ?"

"That I've got a list of possible murderers? One of them did it? Maybe."

"Wow," she breathed.

"So I'll check them out."

"Maybe Brian or Roscoe or Vinnie might recognize them. They've known Daniel a lot longer than me."

"Sure," I said. "These could be names from the war. I'll give those guys a call."

"Hang on," she said. "I'll get their numbers."

She came back onto the line a minute later. She read Brian Sweeney's contact telephone number in Vermont to me. Pollard and Colletti shared the same phone in Turner's Falls, Massachusetts. "Let me know what you find out," she said.

"You can count on it."

"You better be careful, Brady."

"Believe me," I said, "I know how to be careful. Discreet and careful. That's me."

12

The number Cammie had given me for Brian Sweeney was, I remembered, a general store in East Corinth, Vermont. Most likely *the* general store. Gas pumps out front, spinning rods and aluminum lawn chairs and pyramids of maple syrup cans in the window, a wheel of Vermont cheddar and a cracker barrel next to the wood stove, ammunition and knives under the glass counter, cases of beer and sacks of dried beans and bait tanks out back. On the map, East Corinth appeared to be little more than an intersection on the back road from Bradford to Barre, which weren't exactly major metropolitan areas themselves.

"General stow-ah," said the guy who answered the phone when I called Monday morning. "Ed he-ah."

Ed sounded like one of those disillusioned New Jersey dentists who chuck it all and flee to northern New England to pursue their dream of the simple honest country life and end up finding it complicated by leaky roofs, dried-up wells, mud seasons, blackflies, endless winters, suspicious natives, and hard-hearted bankers. More disillusionment.

Generally after a few years they end up practicing rural dentistry.

"I'm trying to get ahold of Brian Sweeney," I told Ed.

"Ain't he-ah just now," said Ed. "Generally comes by lat-ah in the afternoon. I can give him your name."

Ed, I decided, had a poor ear for the significant differences between the Down East Maine inflections—which Hollywood television productions never get right anyway—and those of small-town Vermont.

"My name is Brady Coyne," I said. I spelled it for Ed, and gave him both my office and home numbers. "I'm in Boston. Tell Sweeney to call collect. I'll be at one place or the other."

"Brian'll be by lat-ah," repeated Ed. "He'll want to tell me about the hunting. It's bird season up here now. Pa'tridge, woodcock. Brian's got himself a pair of nice Springers. Hunts all day, don't quit till he's got his limit." Ed tried out a country-boy chuckle. "Heh-heh. Sometimes he don't quit even then."

I managed to disengage myself from Ed only after he told me about how all the male teachers and students played hookey from the regional high school during the first week of the deer season, and how he opened the store at four a.m. that week to sell buckshot and deer urine scent and coffee and sandwiches. I suspected Ed valued the hunters' company as much as their business.

I tried the Turner's Falls number for Roscoe Pollard and Vinnie Colletti. No answer.

I spent the rest of the morning telephone sparring with other lawyers on behalf of clients, and it wasn't until noontime when I found a minute to call Al Coleman in New York. I expected to hear Bonnie's voice on their office answering machine, and I was prepared to leave a strongly worded message. "Where's that damn manuscript?" Something to that effect.

Instead Bonnie answered in person. "The Coleman Literary Agency," she said.

"Oh, hi," I said. "It's Brady Coyne. I didn't expect you to answer."

"I'm back. Just for the week, I hope. Trying to get everything cleaned out. I've gotten all your messages. I would've eventually returned your call."

"Cleaned out?"

There was a long pause before she said, "You don't know, do you?"

"Know what?"

I heard her expel a long breath. "About Al."

"What's going on?"

"Al died."

"Oh, shit. What happened?"

She sighed again. I supected she had been asked that question many times and didn't enjoy answering it. "It was about a month ago. He . . . they said he got mugged."

"Mugged?"

"They found his body in the subway station. He was stabbed. He bled to death. He lay there a long time before somebody figured out that he wasn't a derelict in an Irish linen sports jacket passed out in a pool of blood."

"God!" I managed to mumble.

"New York," said Bonnie Coleman. "I hate this goddam city."

"Look," I said. "You don't have to—"

"It's okay, Mr. Coyne. His clients have to know. I'm turning everything over to Keating and Keating. They're very good. A big Park Avenue agency. It's been a little complicated. See, I'll continue to get the commissions on Al's old accounts, but—you don't need to hear this."

"No, it's all right. I'm not really a client. He had a manuscript."

"Yes, I remember."

"Al had decided not to handle it. He was going to return it—"

"You haven't got it yet?" she said.

"Well, there's no hurry, really. But when you can . . ."

"I don't think I have it."

"Has it been sent? Did it get lost in the mail?"

"I don't know." She paused for a moment. "I don't remember sending it. I—it's been a tough month, Mr. Coyne."

"I'm sorry."

"Yeah." She didn't sound as if she believed me. She must have heard a lot of insincere "I'm sorry"s lately.

"I mean it," I said. "I'm very sorry."

"Okay. Thanks."

"And I'm sorry to be pestering you."

"I assume Al mailed your manuscript to you."

"I haven't got it."

"Wouldn't be the first time the postal service screwed

up. I'll check around. There's still lots of junk here. I'm still finding stuff in the back of the file cabinets. Christ, he kept most of his deals and agreements in his head. I mean, he'd write himself notes, but damned if anybody except him could understand them. You know what I mean? He'd send a proposal to six publishers, and what he'd write down would be the first names of the editors. Then he'd shove the notes under his blotter. I mean, *he* knew what he was doing, but it's been a bear, trying to straighten it all out without him."

"I was just hoping to get that manuscript back."

"What was the title of it?"

"I don't know."

"Well, but . . ."

"And I don't know the author's name, either."

"How . . . ?"

"He used a pseudonym. I don't know what that was. I sent it to Al sealed, just the way the writer gave it to me."

"Well, I'll look for it. I'll see what I can do."

"Thanks," I said. I hesitated. "Bonnie, about Al . . ."

"It's happening all over this city. Which is no consolation. It's a jungle. The police just throw up their hands. A nice quiet little man gets senselessly, randomly murdered, and we're supposed to understand that it's the chance you take, living in this wonderful city. I can't wait to get out of here."

"When did you say it happened?"

"A month ago."

I mentally calculated. It was just about a month earlier when Al Coleman told me that he had decided not to handle Daniel's book. He said he was going to mail Daniel's manuscript back to me. When it didn't arrive, I had tried calling. That's when I began to get answering machine messages.

Al hadn't returned my calls because he couldn't. And Bonnie had other things on her mind.

He died, I figured, before he had the chance to mail back Daniel's manuscript.

"Bonnie," I said, "that manuscript is probably lying around somewhere."

"Probably," she said. "When I find it, I'll ship it along."

"Thanks. Look, if there's anything I can do . . ."

"I've got a good lawyer, Mr. Coyne."

"I mean, as a friend."

"I don't even know you."

"Al and I went to school together."

She laughed softly. "And neither of you remembered each other."

"True," I said. "Still . . ."

"I'm sorry," she said. "I sound rude. I don't mean to be. I've got Al's old friends coming out of the woodwork at me. Most of them want to console me by screwing me. I'm just kinda fed up with guys offering to help, you know?"

"That's not what I meant," I said.

"No, I suppose it's not."

"I guess there really isn't much I could do."

"No, probably not," she said. "I appreciate the thought, though. I'll look for that book."

"Okay. Thanks."

After I hung up from Bonnie Coleman, I swiveled around to stare out my office window down onto Copley Square. The noontime crowds were beginning to swarm over the concrete plaza that separates the public library from Trinity Church. The fountains were turned off, and without them the plaza is pretty stark. But during good weather, secretaries and accountants and sales clerks and stockbrokers mingle there at lunchtime, eating sandwiches from waxed paper on the benches. The men loosen their ties and the women hitch their skirts up over their knees and tilt their faces up to the sun.

On this October Monday they had a crispy autumn day for it. There wouldn't be many more of them.

Somebody murdered Daniel McCloud.

Somebody murdered Al Coleman, too.

Daniel's manuscript was missing.

It seemed to me unlikely that those were unrelated events.

The phone rang just as Julie was pulling the dust cover over her computer terminal for the day. She moved to answer it, but I waved her away. "Go," I said. "I got it."

She hesitated, her hand poised over the console, then smiled and took it back. I reached over and picked up the phone.

"Brady Coyne," I said.

"I have a collect call from Brian Sweeney. Will you accept it?"

"Sure."

"Go ahead," said the operator.

"Brady?" came Sweeney's voice.

"Hey, thanks for calling." Julie kissed my cheek and wiggled her fingers at me. I wiggled mine at her. She left. "Cammie gave me this number," I said to Sweeney.

"I ain't got a phone in my place. I like it that way."

"Sorry to bother you."

"No problem. What's up?"

"Hang on a second. I want to read something to you." I fumbled in my jacket pocket and took out the piece of paper on which I had written the eight names and addresses from Daniel's "insurance" file. "Okay. Got it. Some names. I was wondering if any of them rang any bells with you."

"Names?"

"From Daniel's files. Six of them have photographs that go with them. Cammie didn't recognize any of them. We thought maybe you would. Figured they were friends, acquaintances of Daniel."

"Or enemies, huh?" said Sweeney.

"Yes. Or enemies."

"Okay. Go ahead."

I read them to Sweeney over the phone. When I finished, he said, "Read them again, willya?"

I read the eight names again.

"Nope," he said after a minute.

"You don't know any of these people?"

"Never heard of them."

"Well, okay."

"Sorry."

"Thanks, anyway."

"I didn't know many of Daniel's friends. Just guys from the army."

"And these aren't army names?"

"No. At least, not from when Daniel and I were together. Which was most of it."

"Damn," I said.

"Wish I could help you out."

"Oh, well." I stuffed the paper back into my jacket pocket. "How was the hunting?"

"Daniel wouldn't have approved."

"Why not?"

"I used a shotgun."

"Got some, though, huh?"

"Sure. I always do."

After I hung up with Sweeney I tried the Turner's Falls number again. Roscoe answered. "Yo," he said.

"It's Brady Coyne."

"Who?"

"Daniel McCloud's lawyer."

"Oh, sure. Sorry. What's up?"

"I've got some names. Wondering if they ring any bells with you."

"What kind of names?"

"I found them in Daniel's insurance papers."

"Insurance?"

"Eight names. Six of them have photographs with them."

"So?"

"I don't know. Can I read them to you?"

"Sure. Go ahead."

I did.

"Nope," said Roscoe.

"You don't recognize any of them?"

"No."

"Are you sure?"

"I'm sure, man."

"Brian didn't, either."

"If he didn't know them," said Roscoe, "it's not likely I would. Sweeney and Daniel were tight."

"Is Vinnie there?"

"No."

"Well, would you mind asking him for me?"

"Asking him what?"

"If he recognizes any of the names?"

"Why not? You better read 'em again. If I don't write 'em down, I'll forget."

I read them again, spelling the names.

"Okay," said Roscoe.

"Have him call me." I gave him my phone numbers, office and home.

"If anybody'd know, it'd be Sweeney," said Roscoe.

"He was Daniel's closest friend, huh?"

"As close as the Snake Eater'd let anybody get."

I called Cammie from my apartment that evening. She answered with a cheerful "Hello." I heard music in the background. I recognized a Tom Petty song.

"It's Brady," I said.

"Oh, hi. What's up?"

"Well, for one thing, neither Brian nor Roscoe ever

heard of any of those names. For another, Al Coleman, the guy I sent Daniel's book to, was murdered in New York City and the manuscript is nowhere to be found. Otherwise, nothing's up."

"Murdered? The agent?"

"Yes. Mugged is the verdict. A small statistic. Stabbed to death in a subway station."

"You think . . . ?"

"Quite a coincidence, I think."

"Him and Daniel, you mean."

"Yes."

"Oh, boy."

"Anyway," I said, "I just wanted to let you know. I guess I was hoping maybe you'd thought about those names."

"I thought about them, but I'm coming up blank," she said. "So now what do we do?"

"Maybe I'll try to look up one of these people, see what they've got to say."

"Is that a good idea?"

"Why not?"

"I don't know. Can't do any harm, I guess. The book, though," she said. "I feel bad about that."

"Me, too."

"I've been thinking about it. Now that Daniel's gone, maybe we could get it published with his real name on it."

"I'd like to do that," I said. "I'd like to read it."

"It's missing, though, huh?"

"Al Coleman's wife is trying to find it. But Daniel must have had another copy."

"I can look around." She hesitated.

"He . . . what did you say? He got mugged?"

"Yes. Knifed in a subway station."

"Jesus," said Cammie softly. "What a world."

13

We lingered over coffee while Melissa told us tales of the fifth grade. At recess a boy named David had snatched her Red Sox cap off her head and thrown it up into a playground tree. Another boy, "Old Ross," had shinnied up to retrieve it for her.

"I think David likes me more than Old Ross," she said, looking from Terri to me for affirmation.

"They both like you," said Terri.

"Old David likes you more," I said.

"He's a wicked tease," said Melissa.

"That's how you can tell."

"Which one do you like?" said Terri.

"Oh, Mom. You know."

"Last week it was Kevin."

"Well, it still is. I'm not *fickle,* you know."

Terri darted a glance at me. A *meaningful* glance, although its precise meaning was lost on me.

Melissa abruptly fell asleep in the backseat on the way home from the restaurant to Terri's apartment in Acton.

I carried her up and laid her on her bed. Terri touched the back of my neck, smiled, and mouthed the words "thank you," then bent to undress her. I retreated into the living room. I flicked on Terri's television, but as usual her reception was poor. I turned it off and found some classical music on her radio.

Terri came out in a few minutes. "Drink?"

"Sure. Thanks."

She disappeared into the kitchen. I slouched on her lumpy sofa. I heard her rap the ice-cube tray against the counter. She came back with two short glasses filled with ice and bourbon. She slumped beside me and handed one of the glasses to me.

I held it to her. "Cheers, then."

She touched my glass with hers. "Sure. Cheers."

We sipped. We sat not quite touching. It was Mendelssohn. The *Italian* Symphony. Lush. Romantic. I hummed the theme. Terri poked at the ice cubes in her drink with her forefinger.

"Out with it, woman," I said.

She turned to face me. "Out with what?"

"Whatever it is that Melissa's presence has allowed you to avoid saying to me all evening. That's been on your mind for a month."

She shrugged. "Who said anything's on my mind?"

"Well?"

She nodded. "If I could put it into words I would."

"Don't worry about being articulate. Please try."

She shrugged. "Aw, Brady . . ."

"The thrill is gone, huh?"

She put her hand on my leg. "No," she said. "If the thrill was gone it would be easy. The thrill is still there, and it's been a long thrilling time now, and . . ." Her hand fell away. She shook her head.

"Scary, huh?"

"Not exactly scary. It's . . . uncomfortable for me. It almost hurts. It doesn't fit into my life. It warps everything. It rubs against edges of myself that I didn't know I had."

"Don't you go using that L word on me," I said.

She frowned at me. I smiled, to let her know I was attempting levity. There were times when levity was uncalled for. I usually managed to find those times.

"Damn you," she whispered.

I touched her hair. "Hey," I said. "I'm sorry."

She tilted her head away from my hand. "Don't," she said.

"Try to tell me about it."

"I can't," she said. "It's me, not you."

"The old S word, then."

"Sex? Hardly."

"Space," I said.

She shrugged and nodded. "It's not much of a life," she said, laying her head back on the sofa and addressing the ceiling, "but it's mine, and it works, and it's the only one I know."

"And I've screwed it up."

"No, you haven't. Not yet. And I don't want you to. It just seems inevitable that sooner or later it's got to—I don't know, change, evolve into something else. Something not as good."

"It doesn't have to change."

"Sure," she said. "You'd be happy just to go on and on this way, seeing each other a couple of times a week, sleeping together on the weekend, otherwise just going our own separate ways. And what happens? Where does it go? Nothing stays the same, Brady."

"You're not alluding to the M word, are you?"

"Oh, Christ," she muttered. She laughed quietly. "Look," she said, turning to face me. "If we end it right now, it will always be what it is. It'll always be a thrill. I know you. You'll never get married again. And don't worry, because I don't think I ever will, either. I mean, neither of us has the guts to utter the dreaded L word, never mind the forbidden M word. The way I see it, we've got two choices. We can just bumble along until we get sick of each other and start to despise each other, or we can keep it the way it is by not letting it go anywhere else."

I rolled my eyes. "Makes perfect sense."

"I'm serious. And you don't need to be sarcastic."

I shook my head. "Dames," I said.

She smiled and crept her hand onto the inside of my thigh. She touched my neck, then leaned toward me. The kiss itself was soft and tentative. But Terri's hand moved certainly. "Still a thrill, huh?" she mumbled, her mouth on my throat.

Her fingers went to my belt buckle. I moved to help her, but she pushed my hands aside. "Let me," she said.

We lay together on the sofa long after the *Italian* Symphony ended, Terri's head on my shoulder, our legs entwined.

"We can remember it this way," she whispered.

"I'll miss you."

"Me, too."

"Seems kinda dumb," I said.

"Listen to your head."

"This is all about Daniel, isn't it?"

"I don't know, Brady. All I can tell you is, it's about me. Please don't try to make me explain it."

"You are one complicated broad."

"We all are," she said.

I shuffled through the six photos and two index cards and picked one of the cards. The name on it was William Johnson. It sounded like an alias. He lived at a Summer Street address in Springfield. I dialed information and asked for his phone number.

"I have no William Johnson at that address, sir," said the operator.

"Maybe he has an unlisted number."

"No, sir. Not at that address."

She ended up giving me seven William Johnsons who had phones in Springfield. Between no answers, busy signals, and answering machines, it took me the rest of Monday and most of Monday evening to connect with all seven of them. None of them would admit he had ever lived on Summer Street or heard of Daniel McCloud. Two of them said that Summer Street was in a part of town they wouldn't be caught dead in.

One of those seven William Johnsons, I figured, was

lying. But I had no idea which one, and I didn't know how to pursue it.

The names Daniel had written on the index cards were:

William Johnson
287 Summer St.
Springfield, Mass.

Carmine Repucci
66 Farrow Dr.
Chicopee, Mass.

Chicopee is more or less a suburb of Springfield. The fact that the two index cards carried addresses so close to each other seemed as if it must be significant.

The six photographs, which showed ordinary-looking men of indeterminate middle age, bore this information on the backs:

Boris Kekko
11 Broad St.
Amherst, Mass.

James Whitlaw
422 Hillside Ave.
Pawtucket, R.I.

Mitchell Evans
9 Windsor Dr.
Saratoga Springs, N.Y.

Michael DiSimione
1146 W. Central St.
Providence, R.I.

Bertram Wanzer
2 Hubbard St.
Holyoke, Mass.

Jean Beaulieu
245 River Dr.
Manchester, N.H.

On Tuesday morning I delivered a cup of coffee to Julie
and told her to hold my calls until further notice.

"What's that supposed to mean?" she said. "Further
notice?"

"I've got to make some phone calls. I don't know how
long it'll take. Maybe an hour. Maybe the rest of the morning."

"Trying to scare up a date for the weekend, huh?"

"That's not really funny."

She arched her eyebrows. "Are we having girl problems?"

I smiled, shrugged, and said, "We'll survive."

She narrowed her eyes. Trying to decide whether to
tease me or offer sympathy, I guessed. "You'll grow up," she
said, which wasn't exactly teasing but certainly wasn't the
least bit sympathetic.

"Let's hope not," I said. I pivoted around and strode

to my office. At the door I said, "Until further notice. Remember."

"Poor baby," she said. Teasing, I decided.

I spread the six photos and two index cards over my desk, studied the photos for a few minutes, then turned them over. I observed again that the names and addresses on their backs did not appear to have been written in Daniel's hand, while those on the two index cards did.

I lit a cigarette and reached for the phone.

There was no listing for Carmine Repucci. So much for the two guys on the index cards.

The information operator found no Kekko with a telephone in Amherst.

There were several Whitlaws in Pawtucket, Rhode Island, two named James. One lived at 422 Hillside Avenue.

A woman answered the phone with a cheery "Hello?"

"I'd like to speak to James Whitlaw, please," I said.

"I'm sorry." The cheeriness in her voice had disappeared.

"He's not in?"

"Who is this?"

"My name is Brady Coyne. I'm an attorney, and—"

"Please," she said.

"Pardon me?"

"Mr. Coyne, what is it?"

"I just need to speak to Mr. Whitlaw. I think he has some information for me."

She sighed. "You can't speak to my husband."

"But—"

"Somebody's either playing a dirty trick on both of us, or else you've been misinformed. James died eight years ago."

"Oh" was all I could think of to say.

"What did you really want, Mr. Coyne?"

"I'm sorry," I said. "I'm embarrassed."

"Can I help you?"

"I don't know. Does the name Daniel McCloud mean anything to you?"

She hesitated, then said, "No. I don't think so."

"A friend of your . . . of Mr. Whitlaw?"

"Could be. I don't know. I don't know anybody named Daniel McCloud."

"Can I ask you a question?"

She sighed. "I guess so."

"How did your husband die?"

"He drove his car into a bridge abutment. It exploded. They said he was drunk."

"Oh, gee . . ."

"It was a long time ago, Mr. Coyne."

"Would you mind if I ran a few other names by you?"

"What kind of names?"

"Just to see if you recognize any of them. People your husband might've known or mentioned to you."

"I suppose so."

I read the other seven names and, as an afterthought, added Al Coleman.

"No," she said. "Uh. They don't ring any bells."

"Well, then, I'm sorry to bother you," I said. "Thank you for your time."

"It's okay."

There were half a dozen phone listings for Evans in Saratoga Springs. None lived on Windsor Drive or had the first name of Mitchell.

An entire DiSimione clan lived in Providence, but none lived at 1146 West Central. I jotted down the numbers of the five Michaels, thinking I'd try them later if nothing better turned up.

A man's voice answered Bertram Wanzer's phone in Holyoke. Bingo, I thought. Finally.

"Is this Bertram Wanzer?" I said.

"This is Robert."

"Is Bertram there?"

"No," he said, "the bastard is not here."

"Could I leave a message for him?"

"Look," he said, "what do you want, anyway?"

"I'm a lawyer," I said. "I need his help on a case."

"Well, good luck."

"Can you tell me how I can reach Bertram Wanzer, please?"

"No, I can't."

"Do you mind—?"

"Look, friend. Old Bert walked out on my mother six years ago, okay? No good-bye, no note, nothing. He just fucking left her, not to be heard from since. It took her three years to realize the sonofabitch wasn't coming back. So she divorced him. That's it. He's dead, as far as we're concerned. So when you talk to him, tell him we're doing just fine without him. Better than ever, okay?"

"But you don't know how I can reach him."

"I told you—"

"Yes. I'm sorry. Listen, I didn't know any of this, obviously. Maybe you can help me."

"I doubt it."

"You're Bertram Wanzer's son?"

"His stepson. I don't like to admit it."

"How old were you when he . . . left?"

"Seventeen."

"Do you remember his ever mentioning a man named Daniel McCloud."

"I don't remember much of anything about him. No. No McCloud."

"Are you sure? It's very important."

"I'm sure."

"Is your mother there?"

"She's working."

"Would you mind leaving a message for her? Ask her about Daniel McCloud. If it rings a bell have her call me. Will you?"

He sighed. "Give me your number."

I left my office and home numbers with Robert Wanzer, less than hopeful that I'd ever hear from Bertram's former wife. I scribbled a reminder for myself to try her in the evening.

There were several Johns but no Jean Beaulieu on River Drive or anywhere else in Manchester, New Hampshire. I took down all the numbers for John. I should, I knew, try them all.

But I had lost my enthusiasm for this research. I knew how private investigators did it. They just kept calling.

They'd visit all the William Johnsons in Springfield, all the Michael DiSimiones in Providence. They'd drop in on Mrs. Whitlaw and the former Mrs. Bertram Wanzer, ingratiate themselves, get them talking. Doggedly, mindlessly, they'd keep at it until something turned up.

Private detecting was more painfully tedious, even, than practicing law.

I lit a cigarette and swiveled around to look out my office window.

Eight names from Daniel's insurance file.

I'd taken my best cuts. I had struck out.

I tried Lieutenant Fusco's number. A female cop told me that Fusco wasn't available. I told her to tell him that I had some names that might interest him in regard to the McCloud investigation. She said she'd have him get back to me.

I hung up and buzzed Julie.

"Hi, there" came her voice over the console.

"This is your further notice," I said.

"Goodie. Wanna do some law?"

"Not especially."

"I'll be right in."

Charlie McDevitt and I had lunch at Marie's two days later, which was the first Thursday in November. When the coffee came, Charlie leaned across the table and said, "Well?"

"Well, what?"

"Well, what do you want?"

"Who said I wanted something? Any reason a man can't buy his old roomie lunch?"

"You don't just buy me lunch. We do each other favors and repay them with lunch. Or else we buy the lunch first, thereby creating an obligation. That's how you and I do it."

I lit a cigarette. "A sympathetic ear, maybe."

He cocked his head and smiled. "The beauteous Terri Fiori, huh?"

"She decided to break it off. Before the thrill was gone."

"You're the one who usually does that," said Charlie.

I nodded. "I guess that's true."

"So it must've been easier this time, her doing it."

"Easier, I guess. But it hurt more."

"You ought to settle down, Brady."

"Think so?"

He looked at me. "No, I guess not."

"She did it nicer than I ever could have."

"Give yourself credit," said Charlie. "I bet you made it easy for her."

I shrugged. Charlie and I did not exchange locker-room talk.

"So you're sad. That's good. You'll remember it fondly."

"Boy," I said, "I sure as hell will."

Our waitress refilled our coffee cups.

"You want advice?" said Charlie.

"No, thanks."

"Didn't think so."

"I've been trying to get ahold of Lieutenant Fusco," I said after a minute. "The state cop in charge of Daniel's murder."

"And?"

"He won't talk to me, won't return my calls."

"Why should he?"

I shrugged. "I'm trying to help. I want to know what's happening."

"Hey, Brady," said Charlie.

"Yeah?"

"Forget it."

"Who says?"

"Me. Your friend."

"I said I didn't want advice."

"On matters of the heart, I don't have any useful advice. On stuff like this I do. Whether you want to hear it or not. Forget it. Go practice your law. Last time I looked, you were getting rusty."

"I don't think so," I said.

He sighed, then smiled at me. "Okay. I tried. What can I do?"

"I'd sure like to know who rammed a broadhead into Daniel McCloud's heart."

"Me, too. The cops'll do that for us."

"I got the feeling they won't. I got the feeling they aren't even trying."

"Just because they aren't confiding in you?"

"Partly, I guess. But I'm getting these vibes."

"Yeah. Vibes are good."

"I mean it," I said. "Something's going on."

"Fine. So I repeat. What can I do?"

"I've got some names."

"Names?"

"Cammie gave me Daniel's records. I'm handling the probate for her. Anyway, we found an envelope in with his insurance stuff. It contained six photographs and two index cards. Eight names and addresses."

"Insurance?"

I nodded.

Charlie stared at me for a moment. "And you think one of 'em killed Daniel?"

I shrugged. "There's more. Daniel had written this book, and I sent it to Al Coleman. Remember?"

He nodded.

"Listen, Charlie. At first Al loved Daniel's book. Then a couple of weeks later he called to tell me that he'd changed his mind and was sending the book back. Said he didn't want to deal with Daniel. Sounded almost like he was afraid of him or something. Anyway, the manuscript didn't arrive, so I tried calling to find out where it was. Kept getting their answering machine. Finally last week I got ahold of Al's wife. Bonnie, the girl he used to bring to our place in New Haven. She told me Al got mugged. They found him dead in a subway station."

"Shit." Charlie shook his head slowly.

"This had to've happened sometime shortly after he called me to reject Daniel's book."

"So?"

I shrugged. "Coincidence?"

"Most things are, Brady. What are you getting at?"

"I don't know. I just want to know who killed Daniel, and why. That's all."

"And you think this book . . . ?"

"I don't know what to think. I keep remembering how Daniel's trafficking charges got mysteriously dropped.

That's when he gave me the book. Next thing we know, he and Al Coleman are dead. Now I've got these names . . ."

Charlie stared at me for a minute, then sighed. "Okay. Give me those names. I'll run 'em through the big main-frame, see what I can find out for you."

I nodded. "Good. You've earned your lunch."

I had copied the names onto a sheet of legal-size yellow paper, along with notes from my telephone efforts. I took it from my jacket pocket, unfolded it, and smoothed it out in front of Charlie.

"This Whitlaw died in an auto accident eight years ago," I said. "I talked to his wife. That's the phone number. It's for sure that he didn't kill Daniel. And this Wanzer in Holyoke, he skipped out on his family six years ago, never to be heard from. The rest must've moved or something, because I got no phone numbers for them."

Charlie picked up the paper, folded it, and stuck it into his pocket. "Let's see what we can find out," he said.

"I'm looking for the connection to Daniel."

"Well, hell, I know that."

"This lunch here, it's your payment."

He nodded. "I'll do it," he said. "It doesn't change anything, though."

"What?"

"The advice is golden. You should forget it, Brady."

"I'll consider it."

"Bullshit you will," said Charlie.

14

I called State Police Lieutenant Horowitz at 1010 Commonwealth Avenue that afternoon. He answered his phone with a weary "Yeah. Horowitz."

"It's Brady Coyne. How you doing?"

"Fantastic. But listen. Hearing your voice is still special, you know?"

"I just thought I'd brighten up your day."

I heard him blow a bubble and pop it into the receiver. "So whaddya want?"

"You think the only reason I'd call you is because I want something?"

"Yeah."

"If you wanted something and thought I could help, would you call me?"

"Bet your ass. You owe me."

"Feel free."

"I already do. So what is it?"

"A colleague of yours name of Fusco. Lieutenant Dominick Fusco. Springfield."

"Sure. I know him."

"He's investigating a homicide. The victim was a client of mine."

Horowitz sighed. "So?"

"He won't answer my calls. I want to know how the investigation is going."

"He's probably too busy. You know, investigating homicides."

"I had something I wanted to tell him. Left a message for him to get back to me. He hasn't. He's avoiding me."

"Hard to blame him. If I had as much sense as him, I'd avoid you, too."

"So will you?"

"Will I what, Coyne?"

"Will you find out what the story is? The victim's name was Daniel McCloud."

"Like do they have suspects, have they made an arrest?"

"Yes. Like that."

"Do I get lunch out of this?"

"Absolutely."

"Even if Fusco's got nothing?"

"I just want to know. And I do have some information for him."

He exploded his bubble gum. "I'll get back to you."

He hung up as I was saying "Thanks."

Gloria was perched atop a barstool when I walked into Skeeter's Infield after closing the office for the weekend

Friday afternoon. She was wearing a little black skirt that had ridden halfway up her thighs. She still had great legs.

The rest of her looked equally terrific. Maybe there were a few tiny crinkles at the corners of her eyes and a few strands of gray mixed in with her glossy brown hair that hadn't been there when she took my photograph outside a courtroom in New Haven more than twenty years earlier.

But two kids—now young men—and one divorce later, Gloria Coyne still had it.

I slid onto the stool beside her.

"Hi," I said.

"Hi, yourself." She tilted her cheek for me to kiss, which I did, chastely.

"Been good?"

"You mean my behavior or my health?"

"Either," I said. "Both."

"My health is excellent."

"Otherwise no comment, huh?"

She grinned.

"What are you drinking?"

"White wine, please."

"You used to like gin-and-tonics with a maraschino cherry in the bottom."

She shrugged. "I mostly just have a glass of wine nowadays."

"How about a gin-and-tonic? For old time's sake."

"White wine is fine, Brady. You go ahead and have your Jack Daniel's."

"You used to drink lots of gin. And you'd get all . . ."

"Amorous," she said.

I smiled.

"That's probably why I've just been sticking to white wine lately," she replied.

Skeeter came over and held out his hand. "Hey, Mr. Coyne. How ya doin'?"

I took his hand. "Pretty good, Skeets. You?"

"No complaints. Except for the Sox."

"They need someone who can get from first to third on a single," I said.

"And someone else who can come in from the bullpen and throw strikes. What ever happened to Dick Radatz? What're you folks drinking?"

"Blackjack on the rocks. Lady'll have a glass of white wine."

"No, I think I'll have a gin-and-tonic," said Gloria. "With a maraschino cherry in it."

Skeeter nodded and went to make our drinks. I turned to Gloria. "Thanks for coming."

She shrugged. "It sounded important."

"How are the boys?"

She frowned. "Fine, I guess. They're pretty much men, you know."

"Heard from Billy?"

"Not lately."

"Me neither."

She put her hand on my arm. "You didn't ask me to meet you so we could pool our ignorance about William and Joseph, Brady. What is it?"

"I don't know." I paused to light a cigarette. "I just don't understand women, I guess."

"This is not a revelation to me."

"I know."

"You're looking for insight."

"Yes. After all these years, I suppose I still am."

"Girl trouble, huh?"

I shrugged.

"And you want my advice?"

I looked up at her. "I got dumped."

She grinned. "Welcome to the real world."

Skeeter brought our drinks. I lifted my glass, and Gloria touched it with her gin-and-tonic. "To the real world," I toasted.

Gloria sipped her gin and tonic and smiled.

"Remember Terri?" I said.

"Pretty lady. The boys liked her a lot. Too young for you."

I shrugged. "She didn't think so. Neither did I, actually. Now, maybe, I'm not so sure. Anyway, I had this friend, nice quiet guy living a peaceful country life, with a lady friend who loved him, and he was, um, murdered, and—"

"Murdered," said Gloria. "Aw, Brady."

I nodded. "A tragic, inexplicable thing. Terri has talked a lot with Cammie—Daniel's woman friend—since it happened."

"And then she dumped you."

"Yes. I guess that's what you'd call it. That's the chronology of it. And I just can't help thinking there's a cause-effect relationship between the two events. Daniel getting murdered and Terri ending it with me."

She smiled and shook her head.

"What's funny?" I said.

"You. Men. Your egos."

"Oh. I see."

"Think about it."

I thought about it. "So you're saying . . ."

"You've always been the one to do it," she said. "Starting with me. Right?"

I shrugged.

"So it's happened to you, that's all. Long overdue. Admit it. It's just . . . you. Don't try to make anything more out of it. I know. You'd rather there was some explanation. Something that would allow you to escape with your dignity, or pride, or masculine ego, or whatever it is. The lady dumped you, Brady. She beat you to it. Simple as that."

I sipped my drink. "You're enjoying this, aren't you?" I said.

Gloria shrugged. Then she smiled. "Yes."

After a minute, I said, "It hurts, though, you know?"

She touched my hand. "Believe me, I know."

We finished our drinks. I asked Gloria to have dinner with me, but she said she had a date. I walked her out to her car and held the door for her while she slid in. Her skirt slid way up and she didn't bother tugging it down. I bent in and kissed her cheek. "Thanks for the wisdom," I said.

"Hey," she said, "that's what ex-wives are for."

15

Saturday night. Late. I wondered what Terri was doing. I thought of calling her. I was afraid there'd be no answer at her apartment, though. So I didn't. In keeping with my mood, John Coltrane's sax was blowing "Blue Train" on the stereo. I was at the table by the glass sliders sipping Sleepytime tea and trying to work my way through some back issues of the *Yale Law Review* when the phone rang.

Terri, I thought.

Wishful thinking, I knew.

"It's Cammie," she said when I answered.

"Nice to hear your voice. Everything all right?"

She let out a long breath.

"Hey, are you okay?"

She uttered a sound in her throat. A moan or a sob.

"Cammie, what is it?"

"Oh, shit," she mumbled. "Brady, can you help me?"

"Of course. What's the matter?"

"I almost shot a cop."

"What?"

"It was just a few minutes ago. I had just gone to bed. I heard noises outside. I went to the window. I saw somebody skulking around with a flashlight. I put on a robe and grabbed my gun and I went out onto the porch. He . . . he was right there. He shone his light in my face and I started to point my gun at him and he said he was the police."

"Oakley?"

"Yeah. Him. I never saw his face. But I recognized his voice. He said he was just checking to make sure everything was all right. He said he was concerned for my safety. Because of Daniel, I guess is what he meant. He . . ." Her voice trailed off.

"Maybe he was just doing his job."

"Bullshit." Her voice was harsh. "It's just what Daniel said. Brady, he saw that I had a gun. He'll figure out it's not licensed. I will not give up my gun."

"Maybe you should. What if you had shot him?"

"Are they supposed to come prowling around at night like that?"

"No. Not without telling you first."

"And shining the light like that on me. I know the bastard was . . . looking at me."

"Did he say anything?"

"Just what I told you. I told him to just leave me alone, I was fine. He called me ma'am, polite as pie, tipped his hat, even. Sarcastic, see? Brady, isn't there anything we can do? In court, or something? This has been going on too long. It's not fair."

"I don't know, Cammie. He hasn't really done anything illegal."

"He's been harassing me—us, me and Daniel—since day one. Isn't that enough?"

"Cammie, I'd love to help you—"

"Yeah, but . . ."

"No. Listen. I'll talk to his chief. See if we can straighten it out that way."

"Will you?"

"Sure. Monday. Okay?"

"Thank you."

"In the meantime, keep your doors locked."

"Doors locked and gun handy," she said.

"For Christ sake, be careful."

"Exactly."

I had been to the Wilson Falls police station once before, when I visited Daniel during his weekend in jail. It occupied one wing of the town hall, a no-nonsense square brick building across the village green from the Congregational church.

Chief Francis Padula kept me waiting for fifteen minutes. I sat by myself on a wooden bench and smoked two cigarettes under the watchful eye of the desk sergeant. He didn't even offer me coffee. I knew there had to be a pot of cop coffee somewhere around there.

Finally the chief appeared from a corridor and said, "Mr. Coyne?"

I stubbed out my cigarette and stood up.

He came toward me. He was a compact man in his late thirties with a small mouth and closely cropped hair. He wore a starched white shirt with French cuffs and a blue-and-gray striped necktie snugged tight to his throat. He extended his hand to me without smiling. "Francis Padula," he said.

I took his hand. "Thanks for seeing me."

"Come this way." He turned and I followed him into his office.

He sat behind his desk. I took the straight-backed wooden chair across from him. He folded his hands on the blotter and said, "You were Daniel McCloud's attorney."

I nodded.

"Damn shame," he said.

"Yes."

"I can't talk about the case."

"That's not why I'm here."

He leaned forward and arched his eyebrows. "So what is it?" His eyes were fixed on mine. They were dark brown, almost black. The exact same shade as Terri's, I realized.

"It's about Officer Oakley."

He leaned back. "What about Officer Oakley, Mr. Coyne?"

"I'd rather not file a complaint."

"I'd rather you didn't. Maybe you better explain."

So I did. I related Cammie Russell's complaints to the chief—her perception that Oakley had been harassing her and Daniel for years, how he had arrested Daniel, ticketed the cars of all the guests at the funeral party, and frightened Cammie the previous Saturday night by prowling around the property. Padula studied the ceiling as I talked. I couldn't read his expression. Bored patience or thoughtful concern. One or the other.

When I was done, he said, "I'm not sure I understand your problem."

"You add it all up," I said, "and it's pretty obvious. I mean, ticketing all those cars, for example, while there's a funeral going on."

"All those cars were parked illegally. It's what I instruct my officers to do. Ticket illegally parked vehicles."

"Still. Under the circumstances, it was uncalled for."

"That arrest last summer," he said, "was classic. Perfect police work. I think you know that. You don't think Officer Oakley acted on his own on that one, do you?"

I shrugged.

"Look, Mr. Coyne. Wilson Falls is a small town. I have a small force. When police work needs to be done, there are only a few policemen to do it. Sergeant Oakley is one of them. Any citizen who runs into a police officer here, they're very likely to run into Richard Oakley. Something like that marijuana bust, several of my officers were involved. Oakley was one of them. That's all. It was a good bust."

"So why did the prosecution dismiss it?"

He leaned forward. His eyes bored into mine. He opened his mouth to say something, then closed it. "Ancient history," he said.

"What about the other night? You just can't do that. Skulking around, scaring a citizen like that. It's harassment. I want it to stop."

He shook his head. "Come off it, Mr. Coyne. It's not harassment."

"Maybe a judge should decide that."

He smiled thinly. "And she would have to testify. I'm sure her character is impeccable."

"Look—"

"You know how it works, Mr. Coyne."

"Somebody should've told her that there'd be an officer coming around, at least."

Padula nodded. "That's my responsibility."

"I just want Oakley to leave her alone. Rightly or wrongly, he upsets her. It seems simple enough."

"It's fairly routine to keep an eye on a woman who lives alone after a murder has occurred."

"Sure," I said. "It's good responsible police work. Fine. But it doesn't need to be Oakley. So maybe he hasn't done anything wrong. Maybe it's all in her head. But he spooks her. It doesn't seem necessary. Cammie Russell just wants him to steer clear of her."

"I'll consider what you've told me." He stared at me for a moment. "There's some things you don't know, Mr. Coyne."

"There are lots of things I don't know."

He shrugged.

"Something you should tell me?" I said.

He hesitated, then said, "No. It doesn't matter. I'll speak to Sergeant Oakley." He stood up.

I was dismissed. I reached across his desk to shake hands with him. "Thanks," I said.

He came around the desk as I turned for the door. "Mr. Coyne."

"Yes?"

"Richard Oakley's a good cop."

"Sure."

"He did not murder Daniel McCloud."

"Goodness," I said. "I should hope not."

Fifteen minutes later I pulled into the gravel turnaround in front of Daniel's shop. A cardboard sign hung in the window. CLOSED. I shaded my eyes and peered in. It still looked exactly as it did on the morning I saw Daniel's body in there. I couldn't tell if the bloodstain had been cleaned up.

I walked up the path to the house. I wanted to tell Cammie that I had talked to Oakley's chief. I also needed a mug of coffee.

I rang the bell and waited for her to come to the door. It was one of those gray mid-November New England days when the air is cold and moist and a brittle breeze brings the promise of the season's first snowfall. I shivered and hugged myself in my insubstantial sports jacket. After a minute I tiptoed up to peer through the high window on the door. I saw no lights inside, no sign of life.

I followed the path around the house and continued across the back lawn to Cammie's studio.

There was no bell beside the door. I knocked and called, "Cammie. It's Brady."

I waited. From inside I could hear music, too blurred and faint to identify.

After a minute or two I knocked again. When there was no response, I tried the doorknob. I had told her to keep it locked. But it turned and the door swung open. I stepped inside. "Cammie?" I called.

The woodstove in the middle of the open living room/dining room/kitchen area radiated heat.

Sarah Vaughan was singing "Lover Man."

I didn't see Cammie.

An empty coffee mug sat on the table. A few dirty dishes were piled on the counter beside the sink. The music was coming from the studio upstairs.

"Hey," I called, louder than before. "Cammie? You here?"

I stood there uncertainly, rubbing my hands together beside the woodstove, looking around.

After a few moments I went to the spiral stairway that led up to her studio. As I climbed them the music grew louder.

I stopped at the top step. Skylights and four walls of glass bathed the room in diffuse but bright natural light. I squinted into it for a moment.

Cammie stood at the far end with her back to me. Beyond her through the glass stretched the pewter ribbon of the Connecticut River, winding its way through the umbers and ochers of the late autumn countryside. She was working at an easel. I heard her humming to Sarah Vaughan's music.

She wore cutoff jeans. Her long slender legs were spread wide, as if she were balancing herself on a ship's deck. Her feet were bare. So was her back.

I hesitated at the top of the stairs. It occurred to me to turn quietly and go back down the stairs. Cammie was deep into her work.

She was also virtually naked.

But I did not retreat. I stayed, staring, rooted by the sight of her—the slim perfect line of her legs, the smooth vee of her back tapering into the narrow waistband of her shorts, the pale curve of a breast under her arm, the long black braid bisecting her brown back, the orange ribbon knotted around it.

So I stood there stupidly and watched her, and after a minute she turned slowly around. She held a paintbrush in her right hand, and she had another one clenched between her teeth.

She reached up with her free hand and took the brush from her mouth.

"Hi, Brady," she said quietly.

I nodded. "Hi."

Her breasts were small, perfectly formed. The button on her shorts was open and her fly was half unzipped.

Her eyes glittered and her face shone with her tears.

Sarah Vaughan still sang.

"Cammie, I'm sorry, I—"

She held up her hand. "Don't," she said. She dropped her brushes into a water jar.

She walked toward me. I didn't move.

"Sarah always makes me cry," she said. She came close, reached up her hand, touched my cheek, moved it around to the back of my neck. I felt her other hand slither inside my jacket, move over my shirt against my chest. Her eyes were level with mine. Her mouth was inches from mine. My arms hung at my sides.

Tears continued to overflow her eyes and roll down her cheeks. She took her hand from my neck and peeled off my jacket. Her fingers went to my tie, loosened it, dropped it onto the floor.

"Cammie—"

"Shh," she said. She tilted toward me and kissed me softly on the mouth. She unbuttoned my collar.

I reached up, touched her hands, then gripped her wrists. "No, Cammie," I said gently.

"It's okay." She tried to smile.

"No. It's not." I let go of her wrists and put my arms around her. "It's not okay," I said into her hair. I held her tight.

She burrowed her face against my shoulder. "It's Terri, isn't it?" she mumbled.

"Yes. And Daniel." I hugged her against me. "And us. It's us, too."

We had coffee on the sofa downstairs. Cammie had pulled on a paint-stained T-shirt. Outside, tiny snowflakes had begun to angle down from the leaden sky.

Cammie had replaced Sarah Vaughan with Muddy Waters. He was singing "Sugar Sweet."

"Terri talked to me a lot," said Cammie. "About you. After Daniel died. She likes you a lot."

I nodded. "I know."

"She's pretty confused."

"Aren't we all?"

"Speak for yourself," she said.

"I was."

"Give her time, Brady."

"I think she's made up her mind."

"Minds," said Cammie, "are for changing."

I shrugged. "Terri's very strong-minded."

She nodded. "You're right. Maybe it's better this way anyway."

"That's what I've been thinking."

"I don't know which is worse. Knowing she's there but gone or . . ."

I knew what she was thinking. Or knowing the person you love is dead.

"I talked to your local police chief," I said.

"About Oakley?"

"Yes. I think you'll be okay now."

"Really?"

"This Chief Padula. I think I trust him."

She nodded. "Thank you." She stared out the window for a minute. "What about Daniel's book?"

"I don't know. It hasn't turned up. I guess Al Coleman must've put it someplace. But he's dead, so . . ."

"I've looked all around the house," said Cammie. "Daniel must have kept a copy somewhere."

"No luck, huh?"

She shook her head. "He never talked about it, never shared it. Whatever he was writing, it was a private thing. I never expected him to want to have it published. I figured he was just trying to sort out his feelings. Catharsis—his therapy. When he gave it to you, I was jealous. I mean, he was sharing whatever it was with the world, but not me. I tried teasing him. I even pretended to be angry. But he refused to say anything about it. And after he died, I felt guilty. Do you understand?"

"For giving him a hard time."

She shrugged. "That, yeah. But more for trying to violate his privacy. I mean, if he wanted to keep it from me, he must have had his reasons, and that should have been good enough for me. I'd say, 'Come on, old Snake Eater, gimme a look.' And he'd get that gentle faraway look of his, and he'd say, 'Nay, lass. It's not for your sweet eyes.'" She turned to face me. The tears had begun to well up again. "Ah, shit."

I hugged her. She cried against my chest.

"It's not fair," said Cammie. "I guess that guy—that stranger—and Daniel were the only two people in the world who got to read it. And now it's gone."

"And so," I said, "are both of them."

Cammie heated up some homemade chowder and we watched it snow while we ate. She held me tightly at the door, but she didn't cry.

"Will you come back?" she said.

"Sure," I said.

She tilted back and looked at me. "Thank you."

"For what?"

"For . . . being my friend."

"I'll be back," I said. "I promise."

She kissed me on the cheek.

"And you've got to make me a promise," I said.

"What?"

"Keep your door locked."

She smiled. "I left it open for you."

"How . . . ?"

"I knew you'd stop in. At least I hoped you would."
She shrugged. "I don't know what else I was hoping.
Forgive me. I'm glad we didn't—"

I touched her lips with my finger. "Nothing to forgive," I said.

The snow wet my face as I walked back to my car, and
after I got started it made slush on my windshield. It was
melting on the pavement, but it had begun to stick to the
dead leaves in the oak trees along the roadside.

I expected it would turn to rain as I headed east.

A mile down the road from Daniel's house the cruiser
materialized in my rearview mirror. He switched on the
blue flashers and his high beams at the same time as he hit
the siren. I pulled onto the shoulder and turned off the
ignition. He stopped behind me.

I lit a cigarette. Through my rearview mirror I watched
him step slowly from the cruiser and saunter toward me. It
was Oakley. He paused to peer at my rear license plate. I
rolled down the window. Tiny pellets of snow blew in and
melted against my cheek. He came up to the side of my car
and stood just behind my left shoulder so I couldn't see his
face.

"License and registration," he said.

I found the registration in the glove compartment. I
slid my license from my wallet. I handed the documents to
him. I didn't ask him why he pulled me over. He didn't
offer to tell me. He went back to his cruiser. I smoked my
cigarette and waited.

He was back five minutes later. He bent down to the
open window, braced himself with his hand on the win-

WILLIAM G. TAPPLY

dowframe, and said, "You were going too fast. Roads're wet
and slippery. You've gotta go careful, conditions like this. I
could have cited you. I'm doing you a favor."

Oakley looked older up close. His short dark hair was
liberally flecked with gray, and the skin around his eyes was
puffy and cross-hatched. He was forty-five, give or take a
few years.

He wore a wedding band on the ring finger of his left
hand. For some reason, that surprised me. The only
Richard Oakley I knew was the one Daniel and Cammie
had described for me. It didn't seem likely that anybody
could love that Oakley.

He also had some letters tattooed on the back of his
hand. They were crude and blurred, and they were upside
down to me. But I made them out.

"Semper Fi," they read.

Oakley had been a marine.

He thrust my papers through the window. "Slow
down, okay?"

I took the papers. "Sure," I said. "Thanks."

He hesitated as if he wanted to say something else.
Then he stepped away from my car. "You can go," he said.
"Just drive carefully."

"Yes. Okay."

I pulled away. In my rearview mirror I could see
Sergeant Richard Oakley standing there beside the road,
watching me go.

16

Government Center occupies several city blocks between Cambridge and Congress streets, on the back side of Beacon Hill. It was erected on the corpse of Scollay Square back in the sixties, and there are still some of us who mourn the demolition. Gone is the Old Howard, where a kid could pay two bits to hear a bald man tell dirty jokes and then watch a fat lady strip down to pasties and a G-string. Gone, too, the Blue Parrot, where a teenaged boy could buy a beer, no questions asked, get propositioned by a forty-year-old hooker, and be invited to step into an alley for a fistfight with a sailor, all in the same evening.

Now it's all massive concrete-and-glass buildings and brick plazas. Progress.

Charlie McDevitt's office is high in the J.F.K. Federal Building. I got there around four on Wednesday afternoon. Charlie had called that morning and said he didn't want to talk about it on the phone.

When Shirley, his secretary, saw me walk into the

reception area, she beamed at me. I went over and kissed her cheek. She stood up and hugged me against her great pillowy bosom. "Ah, Mr. Coyne. 'Tis good to see ye."

"You're looking terrific, sweetheart," I said.

Which was true. She had snow-white hair permed into an elaborate do, smooth pink skin, and a healthy abundance of flesh. The prototypical grandma.

"Will ye be takin' him fishin', Mr. Coyne?" she said.

"No, alas," I said. "Fishing season's about ended for the year."

"Maybe come winter some of that silly ice fishing, then."

I nodded. "Maybe."

"Ye should. Himself's needin' some distracting."

"I'll see what I can do."

"Well, go on right in, then. He's expecting you."

I pushed open the door. Charlie was at his desk talking into his phone. He raised his eyebrows when he saw me and jerked his head at the empty chair by his desk. I sat. He rummaged in his bottom drawer and came up with a half-full pint of Early Times. He set it on his desk. I reached over to the sideboard and snagged two water glasses. I poured two fingers into each and slid one of them to Charlie's waiting hand.

Charlie said, "Yeah, okay, get back to me, then," and hung up the phone. He let out a long sigh. "Hey," he said to me.

"Hey, yourself."

He picked up his glass, gestured toward me with it, and took a sip. I did the same.

He rummaged among the papers on his desk top and found a sheet of computer paper. He unfolded it in front of him. "Those names," he said, looking up at me.

I nodded.

"You were hoping to locate them."

"Yes."

"Well," he said, "I located six of them. But it's not going to help you."

"Why not?"

He shrugged. "They're all dead."

I lit a cigarette. "Dead, huh?"

"Yup."

"And the other two?"

He shook his head. "Couldn't locate them."

"Meaning what?"

"Meaning they seem to have disappeared themselves."

"Disappeared?"

"Vanished. Run away. Who the hell knows?"

"Dead, maybe."

Charlie nodded. "Maybe."

I swallowed some Early Times. It burned all the way down. "So what do you think?"

"About the connection with Daniel McCloud, you mean?"

I nodded.

Charlie shrugged. "Well, he's dead, now, too."

"And if these guys are dead—"

"It means they didn't kill Daniel," said Charlie.

"Let's have a look," I said.

He turned the printout around for me. "Mostly FBI

file stuff," he said. "I got a little from the IRS and we even had some data in our own files. I couldn't print it out for you, of course. I'd have twelve G-men with submachine guns pointing at me in about a minute if I did that. But I made some notes and put 'em together for you. What you've got there is a summary. Best I could do. I wasn't sure what you wanted."

I skimmed through it, then went back to the top and read Charlie's notes slowly.

William Johnson. Seven arrests. All drug related. One conviction, served six months at Massachusetts Correctional/Billerica in 1981. His frozen body was found behind a condemned warehouse in Springfield in the winter of 1984. He had been stabbed nine times in the chest and abdomen. He died from the blood loss, not the cold. Assailant unknown.

Carmine Repucci. Small-time thief originally from East Boston. Spent time in prison on three separate occasions, including nine months in Billerica in 1981. His last address was in Chicopee. Found dead in his rented room the day after Christmas of 1987, shot four times in the face and chest. No arrests for his murder.

I glanced up at Charlie. "These first two," I said. "Johnson and Repucci?"

He nodded. "Both crooks. Murdered."

"Daniel had their names on index cards. All the others had photos."

Charlie shrugged. "Yeah? So?"

I shook my head. "I don't know."

"None of the others were murdered," said Charlie.

Boris Kekko. Master's degree candidate in international relations at the University of Massachusetts, Amherst campus. Died of a broken neck in March of 1985 from a fall into an elevator shaft at one of the UMass high-rise dormitories. Charlie had noted in parentheses, "Elevator surfing??" I remembered that game. The kids would get themselves beered up, then jam open the doors and ride up and down on top of the elevator. Sometimes they stepped or fell into the open shaft. Sometimes they fell off the elevator. I remembered Boris Kekko's photograph. He had an open, Slavic face. Balding. Middle-aged. Not a kid.

James Whitlaw. Sales rep for a small computer firm. In August of 1985 Whitlaw drove his Honda Civic into a bridge abutment near Narragansett Bay. The medical examiner's report indicated he had been legally intoxicated. Whitlaw was the one whose wife I had reached.

Mitchell Evans. Professor of comparative government at Skidmore College in Saratoga Springs, New York. Disappeared between semesters in January 1986.

Michael DiSimione, one of the Providence DiSimiones, the crack cocaine lords of New England. Arrested many times, never indicted. Had agreed to testify before a Senate committee in return for immunity and admission in the Federal Witness Protection Program when, in October of 1986, he apparently changed his mind and shot himself behind his right ear in a New York City hotel room.

Bertram Wanzer. Software engineer for a now defunct electronics firm in Holyoke. Disappeared sometime in the summer of 1987, divorced by his abandoned wife three years later. I had talked with his stepson Robert.

Jean Beaulieu, independent trucker, accidentally

drowned in the Merrimack River south of Manchester, New Hampshire, on July 4, 1989 when intoxicated.

I looked up at Charlie. "Jesus," I said.

He shrugged.

"What do you make of it?"

"I don't know," he said. "Six of 'em are dead."

"Maybe all eight," I said.

He nodded. "Could well be."

"And now Daniel."

"He'd make number nine," said Charlie.

"And you might add Al Coleman to the list." I lit a cigarette and stared out Charlie's office window. "Except for their all being dead—or at least six of them, not counting Daniel and Coleman—what's the connection?"

"You tell me."

"Let's play with it."

"Well," he said, "they're all males."

I nodded impatiently. "Yeah, okay. Something else, though."

"I can't see it," said Charlie. "Except they were all on Daniel's list."

"Which means they *are* connected. Daniel knew what it was."

Charlie swiveled his head to look at me. "His book?"

I nodded. "That'd be my guess. He was researching something, and found it. Whatever it was, these names are the key." I shook my head. "If they were all murdered, or all crooks, or all in the same business, or something, it might start to make sense."

"Or if they were all born in the same hospital, or went to the same school. They knew each other. Were friends."

"Or enemies."

"Or had the same enemy."

"They all fucked the same woman," I said.

"Christ, Coyne," said Charlie. "Maybe they were all veterans. In the army together."

"Not with Daniel they weren't," I said. "Brian Sweeney already checked that out." I snapped my fingers. "Agent Orange victims, maybe. Like Daniel."

"Maybe they were all those things," said Charlie. "Or some combination. Into something together. There's gotta be a connection."

I stared down at the printout. "Well," I said, "I don't see it here."

"I can dig a little more."

"Yeah?"

He shrugged. "Why not?"

"You want me to buy you lunch or something?"

He waved his hand impatiently. "I'm as curious as you are. Daniel was my friend, too."

"His book," I said. "Wish I could lay my hands on it. He knew something."

"Bet your ass he did."

"And he got murdered," I said. "And so did Al Coleman."

"Seems like more than coincidence, doesn't it?" said Charlie.

17

After a microwaved TV dinner that evening—chicken, green beans, mashed potatoes, and gravy—I unfolded Charlie's printout onto my dining-room table. I took turns reading the dim dot-matrix printing and staring out the sliding glass doors at the dark harbor six floors below my apartment building.

There were a few lights blinking down there on the cold black water.

Not many lights flickered in my cold black brain. At least, none that helped me to see who killed Daniel McCloud.

I saw some isolated connections on the list. The two guys on index cards, the names without photographs, William Johnson and Carmine Repucci, were the only two who had been murdered. Both had spent time at M.C.I./Billerica in 1981, both were small-time hoodlums, both ended up living in the Springfield area. Most likely they knew each other.

There was a student and a professor. International relations and comparative government were both specialties in political science.

There was a computer sales rep and a software engineer. Same industry.

There was one suicide, but it was possible that Jean Beaulieu, the trucker who drowned, made two.

Two had disappeared. It was logical to hypothesize that they, like the others on the list, were dead.

None of the deaths was by natural causes. Not counting the two disappearances, there were one suicide, two murders, and three accidents.

A clever killer can make his work look like a suicide or an accident. If he succeeds in hiding a dead body, he can make it look like a disappearance.

All eight could have been murders.

What had Daniel learned?

Did his name belong on that list? Number nine? That's where it belonged chronologically.

Or make it ten. Al Coleman probably belonged on the list, too.

Say that. Say ten connected deaths. Say all were murders.

Say there were ten murders by a single killer.

Then whoever murdered the eight also murdered Daniel and Al.

Solve one crime. That solves them all. Including Daniel's.

Clouds scudded across the full moon outside my window, momentarily giving me a peek at it before they moved in front of it again. The Beaver Moon, I recalled idly. Where the hell did it get a name like that? I could get out the *Old Farmer's Almanac* and look it up.

If I had Daniel's book, I believed I could look up the answer to the question I really cared about: Who murdered him?

Charlie called me the next afternoon. "Something weird's going on," he said without preliminary.

"Tell me."

"I was about to." He hesitated. "I can't punch up those names on my computer anymore."

"What do you mean?"

"Shit, Brady, wasn't I clear? I came in this morning and tried to get back into those files. They're not there. Ours, FBI, IRS. Gone. They were there a couple days ago. Now they're not."

"So—?"

"So how the hell do I know? These computers are screwed up half the time. Still, it's weird."

"Charlie . . ."

"Look," he said. "Before, I was just pretty much humoring you, trying to satisfy your curiosity. Because we're friends and I admire your . . . whatever, your tenacity, your singleness of purpose, even if your purposes sometimes elude me. And I guess I figured maybe we both owed it to Daniel. Now I'm curious myself. So you don't even have to tell me. I'm going to see if I can find out what's going on here. I'll be in touch."

Charlie hung up without saying good-bye.

• • •

I stayed at the office after Julie closed up shop, and I reached the former Mrs. James Whitlaw in Pawtucket around six. She answered with a breathless "Yes?"

"Mrs. Whitlaw?"

"Yes. Goodness. I ran for the phone. Who is this?"

"It's Brady Coyne calling again."

"Who?"

"I called you a while ago. I was looking for your husband."

She was silent for a moment. Then she said, "I'm sorry . . . ?"

"I'm a lawyer. You told me about Mr. Whitlaw's death."

"Oh. Yes, I remember."

"Would you mind answering a couple of questions for me?"

"Look, Mr. Coyne—"

"It's very important."

"Does this have anything to do with his . . . the accident?"

"In a way, yes, it does."

"Because I never believed it, you know."

"Believed what?"

"That he was drunk when he crashed."

"No?"

"No. Oh, James might have a beer now and then. But he was not a drinker. And he was a very careful person. Not wild. Not at all. He was actually . . . most people thought of him as rather boring. Actually, he was. Boring. But he was steady and he was a good man. He always used his seat belt, and he just wouldn't get into a car and drive if he'd had more than one beer."

"So you think . . . ?"

She laughed quickly and without humor. "I don't think anything anymore. It doesn't really matter, does it?"

"Maybe it does, Mrs. Whitlaw." I glanced down at the pad of yellow legal paper where I had scratched some reminders. "May I ask you a few questions?"

"I don't see any harm in it, I guess."

"Did your husband attend college?"

"Yes. The University of Connecticut."

"What did he major in?"

"Business administration. He started for his master's but didn't finish."

"Was he in the service?"

"Oh, yes. The lottery took him from graduate school."

"Was he in Vietnam?"

"Yes. He was wounded."

"Wounded?"

"A mine. He lost three toes. He walked with a limp. He was quite self-conscious about it."

"Did he ever encounter Agent Orange over there?"

"No, I don't think so."

"Was he by chance in the Special Forces?"

"Huh?"

"The Green Berets?"

"Oh. No. He was a marine lieutenant. All that was a long time before I met him, Mr. Coyne. He told me all these things. We were only married for two years when he . . ."

"Yes," I said. "I'm sorry."

"He told me all about his life. He had had a hard life. We were very happy, the time we had."

I cleared my throat. "I'd like to read some names to you, see if you recognize any of them."

"You mentioned other names to me when we talked before, didn't you?"

"I guess I did. Can I do it again?"

"Well, okay. I'm not sure I was really paying attention before."

I read the other seven names to her. I added Daniel's name onto the end.

"Hmm," she said. "I don't know."

"Want me to read them again?"

"Yes."

I did.

"No. Some of the last names. Evans, Johnson. But not with the same first names."

"These might've been men your husband knew, names he could've mentioned to you."

"It was a long time ago."

"People he might've known in the war."

"He didn't like to talk about the war."

"Sure." I hesitated. "I have a different question."

"All right."

"Mrs. Whitlaw, was your husband ever in trouble with the law?"

She paused. "I don't see . . ."

"It's important," I said.

"I don't know. I didn't know him for very long." She stopped. "Who are you, anyway?"

"I told you. My name is—"

"I don't think I should talk to you anymore."

"Mrs. Whitlaw—"

She hung up on me.

The other connection I had made was with Robert Wanzer, Bertram's stepson. Wanzer was the software engineer who had abandoned his wife. She had eventually divorced him in absentia. Young Robert, I recalled, was still angry.

He answered the phone with a grumbly "H'lo?"

"Is this Robert Wanzer?" I said.

"Yuh."

"This is Brady Coyne again. I spoke to you last week."

"You were looking for my stepfather."

"Right. You explained what happened. I wonder if you'd mind answering a couple of questions for me."

"I'd mind," he said. And he hung up.

I held the dead phone against my ear for a moment, then put it back onto its cradle. I figured I could learn something from the folks who made a living soliciting over the telephone. I was two for two in getting hung up on. Not a winning percentage.

I gave Robert Wanzer the time it took me to smoke a cigarette, then called again.

"H'lo?" he said.

"Your stepfather did not abandon your mother," I said quietly.

"Who the hell *are* you, anyway?"

"I told you—"

"Yeah, right. So what are you talking about?"

"I believe he was murdered."

There was a long silence.

"Mr. Wanzer, are you there?"

"I'm here," he said. "You better explain yourself."

"It's too complicated to explain," I said. "You'll have to trust me."

"Why should I?"

"What've you got to lose?"

"Hm," he said. "Right. Good point. What do you want to know?"

"I have some questions about Bertram Wanzer."

"You don't think he ran off?"

"No."

"Why?"

"If you'll answer my questions, maybe I'll be able to answer yours better. Okay?"

"Go ahead."

I asked him the same questions I had asked Mrs. Whitlaw. I learned that Bertram Wanzer had earned a bachelor's and master's at MIT in math. He had never been in the service. He had been arrested several times in the sixties and early seventies for demonstrating against the war and in favor of civil rights. He settled down, got a job, married. Then, without warning, he disappeared.

"This is what he told us," said Robert. "This all happened before my mom met him. I was a kid when he came along. He adopted me. He was like a father. I called him Dad. They were good years. The best of my life. My mom's, too. Then . . ."

"Mr. Wanzer," I said, "I'd like to read some names to you, see if they ring any bells with you."

"What kind of bells?"

"People your stepfather might've been associated with. Friends of his. Business acquaintances. Just names he might've mentioned."

"I was only seventeen when . . ."

"Let's try."

"Okay."

I read the seven other names plus Daniel's.

"Sorry," he said.

"Are you sure?"

"I'm sure I don't remember any of them. He might've mentioned them or something, but I don't remember it."

"Would you mind copying them down and running them past your mother?"

"I guess that'd be okay."

I read them to him, spelling them. Then I gave him my phone numbers, office and home.

"Let me know," I said. "Anytime."

"Sure."

"Even if she comes up blank."

"I'll call you," he said. "Can I tell her that my stepfather was murdered?"

"I'm not positive he was," I said. "But I think so. If you think it'll make her feel better . . ."

"It will," he said. "Guaranteed."

18

I tried to call Charlie the next morning, but Shirley told me that he was out of the office. I asked her to have him call me.

I tried Horowitz. He was out, too. So I spent the morning practicing law. Julie told me that I needed the practice.

Charlie called around noon. "Let's have lunch," he said.

"Good. I got some thoughts."

"Me, too. Meet you at Marie's in an hour."

He was at our usual corner table when I got there. I took the chair across from him and said, "What're you drinking?"

"Tap water."

"Looks good."

Our waitress, a BU undergraduate named Rita, came over and said, "Hi, Mr. Coyne. Want a drink?"

"I'll have the same as my uncle."

"It's one of our specialties," she said.

When she left, I said, "Listen, I got some hypotheses. Want to hear them?"

Charlie nodded. "Go ahead."

"I talked to the widow Whitlaw and Bertram Wanzer's son last night. Looking for commonalities. Wanzer got arrested a few times for civil rights and antiwar stuff, and when I asked Mrs. Whitlaw if old James had ever had a problem with the law she hung up on me, which answered that question. Then there was that DiSimione in Providence, who was a candidate for the Witness Protection Program. A big-time hood, obviously. Add to that the two small-timers who got murdered in Springfield, Johnson and Repucci, and we've got all five in trouble with legal problems of one sort or another. That's five for five that we know of. We also know Daniel got arrested on that marijuana thing, so if the other three on the list . . ."

I let my voice trail off. Charlie was rotating his water glass between the palms of his hands, staring down into it as if he'd noticed bugs swimming there.

"Hey, Charlie?"

He looked up. "I've been listening, Brady."

"What d'you think?"

He shrugged. "Anything else?"

I flapped my hands. "Shit. I thought that was interesting enough. Okay. The other thing is a possible connection to Vietnam. We know about Daniel. This Whitlaw—he was a marine, not SF, but he got some toes blown off over there. Wanzer evidentally stayed home. But he was an active protester. Check this thought: Daniel was bitter about his getting Oranged, Whitlaw, maybe, was equally pissed at losing some digits, and Wanzer opposed the war anyway. If the others—Charlie, what the hell is the matter today?"

He wasn't looking at me. It was hard to tell if he had even been listening. He slouched across from me playing with his glass and staring down at the table.

His head came up. "Brady, I gotta tell you something."

I shrugged. "Go for it."

At that moment Rita delivered my glass of water. "Ready to order?" she said.

"I'll try the cannelloni," I said.

"Just a bowl of minestrone," said Charlie.

"Wine?"

"No," said Charlie. "Thank you."

Rita smiled and left. Charlie gazed off in the direction she had taken. I sensed that he wasn't really focusing on how gracefully Rita's slim hips rolled in her tight jeans.

He turned to face me. "Neighbor of mine, guy named Lewis, Jimmy Lewis, he's got this beagle. It's just a pet, his kids' dog, really. They call him Snoopy. Anyways, my neighbors on the other side are this middle-aged couple named Tomchik. Quiet folks. No kids. But they've got a pet rabbit called Daisy, one of those expensive breeds with long fur and big floppy ears. Daisy is like their kid, okay? You know how childless couples can be with their pets. I mean, they keep this bunny in a cage out back, but they like to bring her into the house, feed her table scraps, take her for a ride in the car, even. Okay, the other evening Jimmy

Lewis comes over. He's looking kinda upset. I give him a drink, ask him what's up. He says he wants to talk to me. I say sure, go ahead. Seems that the other day Snoopy the beagle comes marching into the house and he's got Daisy the rabbit in his mouth. Old Daisy's stone-dead, all covered with dirt and dog drool and whatnot. Jimmy's visibly upset, telling me this. He says, 'So what would you have done, huh?' I shrug. I figure he's about to tell me what he did and he just wants me to tell him he did the right thing."

Charlie paused to sip his water. I took that opportunity to say, "Um, Charlie? Is there a point to this? Because we've got some important things to discuss here."

He waved his hand. "Bear with me. Jimmy says he knelt down and told Snoopy 'good dog' and patted his head and took Daisy's corpse from his mouth. He says to me, 'Shit, Charlie. The Tomchiks loved that stupid bunny. How in hell am I gonna tell 'em that my dog killed Daisy, huh? They'll hate me forever.' So Jimmy takes Daisy to the kitchen sink and washes all the mud and shit off her, then brushes her and fluffs her with a hair drier."

"A hare drier?" I said.

Charlie shrugged. "Sure. Pun optional. Anyway, after it gets dark he sneaks into the Tomchiks' backyard with Daisy under his arm. He sticks her into her cage, latches it, and skulks back home. He's telling me this, and he says, 'See, Charlie, I figure they'll assume old Daisy had a stroke or something, died peacefully, looking all clean and pretty the way they keep her. No harm done, right?' And I nod to him. Sounds good to me."

"You going somewhere with this?" I said.

"Almost there," said Charlie. "Jimmy says a couple days later he runs into Mrs. Tomchik at the market. They exchange greetings, the way neighbors do, how've you been, your yard's looking nice, stuff like that, and Mrs. Tomchik gives Jimmy this mournful look and says to him, 'I guess you didn't hear.' And Jimmy says innocently, 'Hear what?' And she says, 'We had a death in the family.' And Jimmy's saying, 'Oh, shit,' to himself, because he knows how much those people loved that dumb rabbit. And she says, 'Yes. Poor Daisy has passed on.' And Jimmy says, 'My sincere condolences. I hope it was painless.' And she says, 'Yes. We think Daisy must've had a heart attack. But the strangest thing happened.' 'What's that?' says Jimmy. 'Well,' says the woman, 'we buried her, of course. And then somebody dug her up and cleaned her off and put her back into her cage.'"

Charlie folded his hands on the table and peered at me.

"You're trying to tell me something," I said.

He nodded.

"It's pretty oblique."

He shrugged.

"Okay," I said. "I get it. But I don't understand. Yesterday you were hot to figure out what happened to Daniel McCloud, and now you're saying we should leave dead rabbits where they're buried, or something to that general effect."

"Something," said Charlie, "to that precise effect. Listen," he said, leaning toward me and grabbing my wrist, "as your best and most trusted friend, who profoundly hopes we'll slip into our golden years together, you and I, casting Pale Morning Duns at rising brown trout in Rocky Mountain rivers and slicing golf balls into sand traps on all the great courses in the world, I'm saying to you: Forget it. Okay? Leave it be. Daniel's dead. Irrevocably dead. Nothing anybody can do about it. It's a shame, but it happens. One way or the other, it always happens."

I pulled my wrist out of his grasp. "What the hell is the matter with you?" I said.

"Come on, Brady. I mean it. You keep doing this, and it's time you outgrew it."

"Doing what?"

He waved the back of his hand around in the air. "This," he said. "This . . . amateur detective work. This poking your nose into places it doesn't belong."

"Don't you care what happened to Daniel?"

Charlie shrugged. "I wish he was still alive, if that's what you mean."

"What about whoever murdered him? Don't you want to see him fry?"

He shook his head slowly. "Justice, you mean. You want justice."

"Yeah. Justice."

"Brady, what is it? Really? Why do you keep glomming onto these things like a big old snapping turtle with a stick in its mouth, shaking your head around and refusing to let go? And don't give me that justice crap. Anybody who went to law school knows better."

I sighed. I shook a Winston from my pack and lit it up. "You're asking a serious question?"

Charlie nodded. "A serious question. Yes."

"Shit," I said. "We've talked about this before. You know me. I just like knowing things. Or maybe I should say, I don't like not knowing. Call it a character defect, if you want. I can't help it. I'm impatient with the mysterious ways of nature or life or God or whatever you want to call it. Some great Catholic theologian once said, 'Whatever is, is to be adored.' Well, I think that's bullshit. 'Whatever is, is to be *understood*.' That's my motto. That's what this is all about, being alive and human. Trying to figure things out. Wanting to know things that you don't know. Listen. You're always giving me this line, Charlie. Fine. I expect it. But you never really mean it. Tell the truth. I think you kinda like it when I go banging around trying to understand things. Right? You usually try to help me. Now you're different. Now I got the feeling here that you really do mean it. What's up?"

"Teilhard de Chardin," said Charlie. "The theologian. Whatever is, is to be adored. God's way. Go with the flow. Comforting wisdom, that."

"It doesn't comfort me."

Charlie shrugged. So did I.

Rita brought our food. Charlie hunched over his soup. I attacked my cannelloni. We didn't talk. Charlie slurped about half of his soup, then put down his spoon and pushed the bowl away.

"You all right?" I said.

He shrugged.

"Hey. Marie makes the best minestrone in the city."

"My stomach's been a little off lately."

I nodded. "That explains it, then."

"What?"

"Your gloom. All these negative emanations zipping out of your skull. Whaddya say, Charlie. Let's figure this sucker out, huh?"

"No, Brady. Please. Forget it."

"Come on, old buddy. You perform some computer tricks, and I'll do some pinching and tickling, and we'll see who squeals and giggles. Whaddya say?"

He shook his head. "I'm serious, Brady."

I stared at him. He lifted his gaze to meet mine. "You really are, aren't you?" I said.

He nodded. "Yes. Back off. Do what I tell you."

"Well, fuck it, then," I said.

"You'll back off?"

"Shit, no. I'll just have to do it without you."

19

I walked back to Copley Square from Marie's in Kenmore with the collar of my jacket turned up against the November chill. But I was more chilled by Charlie than by the weather. He was always telling me to grow up and mind my own business. But he never really meant it. Charlie, as a prosecutor for the Justice Department, had plenty of opportunity to nose around in crime and mystery. It was his business, and he enjoyed it, and he understood why I sometimes found myself trying to figure out who had cheated, robbed, extorted, and occasionally even murdered my clients or their friends and relations.

We always joked about it. Lawyers do that. If law school doesn't make you cynical, the practice of law quickly does.

Lawyers rarely admit they're committed to justice. They never admit it to each other. We talk mostly about billable hours, sometimes about winning. Among ourselves, we call the law a business and ourselves businessmen.

But most of the lawyers I know still nurture the vestige of what got them into law in the first place. The quest for an abstraction. Justice.

Ever since the day I met him at Yale, Charlie McDevitt had always dreamed of a seat on the Supreme Court. With Charlie, it was never prestige. It was the ultimate opportunity to make justice.

Now something in him had changed, and it worried me.

But it didn't change my mind.

When I got back to the office I called Horowitz at the state police barracks. When he answered the phone I said, "You get ahold of Lieutenant Fusco yet?"

"Ah, shit," he said. "I told you I was gonna do that, didn't I?"

"You promised."

"What was the question?"

"The Daniel McCloud murder in Wilson Falls."

"Right." He popped his bubble gum. "Okay. I seem to recall there was a lunch in this for me."

"There was, yes."

"Where?"

"You name it."

"I will."

"Couple of things, while you're talking with Fusco," I said.

"I wouldn't push too hard, Coyne."

"I called him a while ago. Had some names I thought he might want to check out."

"Names?"

"Maybe connected to the McCloud murder."

"And?"

"And he never called me back. I'm just trying to cooperate."

"Hm," said Horowitz doubtfully.

"Anyway," I said, "along the same line, there's something specific you can mention to him when you talk to him. Okay?"

"Go ahead."

"Just a couple of old crimes out near Springfield that Fusco might know something about. Got a pencil?"

"I've got a pencil, for Christ's sake," he growled.

"Okay. One, William Johnson, murdered in 1984. Two, Carmine Repucci, murdered in 1987."

"So what's the question?"

"Mainly, if and how the two of them might be connected. They were both small-timers, spent time in Billerica. I'd like to know if they were there at the same time, maybe cellmates. Were they partners when they got out? I'd like to know if they were in Vietnam, or in the service at all, and if so, when and where. I want to know if anyone's been prosecuted for their murders, or suspected but not prosecuted, or what."

"What you want to know," said Horowitz, "is how either of these two guys might be connected to your McCloud. Right?"

"What I really want to know," I said, "is if the same person killed all three of them."

"This'll be one helluva lunch you're gonna owe me, Coyne. But, yeah, lemme see what I can find out."

"When?"

"When what?"

"When are you going to see what you can find out?"

"I can't do it while I'm talking to you, can I?"

"Nope."

After I hung up with Horowitz I began to rummage among the neat stacks of paper that Julie had assembled on my desk, and before I knew it she was poking her head into my office and telling me she was leaving. I wished her a pleasant weekend and returned to my paperwork. She stood in the doorway for a minute beaming at my diligence, and I wondered if she had talked to Charlie. Julie would like it if she thought I had overcome my childish obsession with unbillable hours.

At five-thirty Horowitz called. "Meet me at Hilary's in fifteen minutes," he said.

"You mean please?"

"No. Meet me."

"Okay."

After I hung up I reorganized the stacks of paper on my desk. There was a new stack now. Stuff I had done. It wasn't very tall. But I was proud of it.

I switched on the answering machine, got my jacket, locked up, and left. J. C. Hilary's is across the square from my office building. Horowitz had chosen it for my convenience, which wasn't characteristic. And when I thought about it, I realized it was uncharacteristic of him to meet me at all. Usually he'd tell me what he'd learned over the telephone.

He must've learned something.

I found a booth and ordered a bourbon old-fashioned. I sipped at it and smoked cigarettes and watched the Friday evening bar crowd tell loud stories and flirt with waitresses, and I was halfway through my second drink before I saw Horowitz shoulder his way toward me. He was three-quarters of an hour late.

He slid into the booth across from me. "Traffic," he muttered.

"I thought cops were never bothered by traffic. Flick on the siren and the flashers and everyone pulls over to let you by."

"Shit," he said. "Flick on the siren and the flashers and everyone ignores you. I need a beer."

He looked around and caught the eye of the waitress. She nodded to him and in a minute or two she came over. "Sir?"

"Gimme a light beer."

"We've got Coors, Mich, Bud, Miller."

Horowitz waved his hand. "Michelob, I guess."

He stuck his forefinger into his mouth and removed a wad of chewing gum. He put it into the ashtray. He looked up at me from under his shaggy black eyebrows. "Coyne," he said, "I got instructions for you."

I rolled my eyes. "Goodie."

"Leave cop work to the cops."

"This from Fusco?"

He leaned toward me. "This is from me. All you do is annoy people. You take up their time. You get in the way. You do more harm than good. You—"

"I've heard it," I said quickly. "You're trying to tell me

that Fusco doesn't have anything, that they're making no progress on the McCloud case."

He shrugged. "That's true, but—"

"And everyone's embarrassed at their incompetence and they don't want the civilians to know it."

"Listen," he said. "There's things you don't know."

"Hey," I said. "A revelation."

"Dammit, Coyne. I'm talking to you as a friend here."

"That's a first."

He stared a me for a moment, then lowered his eyes and shook his head slowly back and forth. "I mean it," he muttered.

"About being my friend?"

"No. About putting down your fucking lance and leaving the windmills to us."

The waitress brought his beer and said to me, "Another, sir?"

"No," I said. "I've got to stay sharp so I can figure out what my friend here is trying to tell me that he won't say."

She frowned, then shrugged.

After she left, Horowitz said, "Okay, Coyne. I'm gonna be straight with you."

"Another first."

"The McCloud case is on the back burner."

"You mean they've buried it."

He shrugged.

"Why?"

"Can't tell you."

"Do you know?"

"I got an idea."

"This Fusco's doing?"

"No."

"Somebody higher than Fusco, then."

"Look," said Horowitz, "I shouldn't have told you that much, okay? Except I am trying to impress upon you the importance of your backing off."

"As a friend."

"Sure," he said. "As a friend. Okay?"

"I don't get it."

"You don't have to get it, Coyne. You're not supposed to get it. You're just supposed to do it. Go argue alimony, or whatever it is you do."

"And leave cop business to the cops."

"Yes."

"Except they're not doing it."

He blew out a long sigh. "Call it a warning. Call it advice. Call it whatever you want. Just tell me you hear me."

"I hear you," I said.

He sighed deeply. "Good."

"I will take it into account."

"You pigheaded son of a bitch," he said.

"What about Johnson and Repucci?" I said. "Learn anything about them for me?"

"If I tell you will you get the McCloud bug out of your ass?"

I stared up at the ceiling, pretending to ponder. "Okay," I said. "It's a deal."

"Mean it?"

"Sure." It was a lie, but it didn't bother me.

He stared at me for a moment. "Okay," he said.

"Johnson and Repucci both did time at Billerica in 1981. Their sentences overlapped by about three months, and they were in the same cellblock, so they undoubtedly knew each other. Johnson got out first and turned up in Springfield. Repucci grew up in Eastie, and that's where he got arrested. When he got out, he went to Chicopee, which, as you know, is right next to Springfield. Whether him and Johnson worked together or not I couldn't tell you. Logical assumption, though. They were both fringies, well known by the police, pulled in several times, but never charged with anything. When Johnson got offed, they questioned Repucci about it, but nothing came of it. They never made any arrests on Johnson's murder. Guess they assumed it was a territory thing. Drugs, hookers, protection. One less asshole on the streets. You know how it works."

Horowitz shrugged. I nodded.

"Anyways, Repucci got it a few years later. Same deal. The assholes want to knock each other off, saves us all a problem."

"So neither murder was solved," I said.

"Right," said Horowitz. "No arrests, even."

"You check on their war records?"

"Neither of 'em was ever in the service."

"They don't sound like the kind of gentlemen who'd march for peace."

He shrugged. "They weren't arrested for it. That's all I can tell you." He picked up his beer and took a small sip.

"That's it?" I said.

"That's all."

I fumbled in my jacket pocket and found the printout

Charlie had given me. I unfolded it and put it in front of Horowitz. He glanced down at it, then looked up at me. "What's this?"

"Some names."

"Christ," he said. "I can see that."

"Johnson and Repucci are on this list. This is what I wanted to tell Fusco about. There's some connection among all of them. Plus Daniel McCloud."

Horowitz picked up the printout and, without looking at it, refolded it and handed it back to me. "I told you already," he said. "And you promised."

"You won't check them out for me?"

"Absolutely not. And don't you, either."

I tucked the printout into my pocket. "Right," I said. "I promised."

20

The shrill of the telephone beside my bed popped my eyes open. Seven o'clock. My brain reluctantly ground into gear, and the vise around my temples reminded me of two more bourbon old-fashioneds at Hilary's after Horowitz left, then a steak, then stopping at Skeeter's on the way home where I watched the basketball game and argued with a guy who didn't think Bob Cousy could even break into the starting five for Holy Cross in the new era of basketball.

I'd had a few beers at Skeeter's. The Celtics won, and I believed I won my argument, too, and so I'd celebrated with a mug of coffee laced with Jack Daniel's.

Skeeter had made sure I wasn't driving before he gave it to me.

And throughout the evening, on the level beneath the basketball and the booze and the fellowship of the bar, the question festered in my brain: Why had first Charlie and then Horowitz, two trusted friends, both been so humorlessly earnest in warning me off the Daniel McCloud case? Both of them had indulged me plenty of times in the past, no questions asked, no judgments rendered.

And now, at seven a.m., too damn early on a Saturday morning, my phone was ringing. What now?

I got it off the hook and against my ear. "Yuh?"

"Hey, Pop. You awake?"

I groaned. "I am now." Joey. My younger.

"Well, say hi to Terri for me."

"Huh?"

"Terri. Listen. Feel around. She's the one beside you."

"There's nobody here but me."

"Yeah?"

"Yeah."

"Something wrong?"

"Nothing's wrong. She's not here. We're not together these days."

"Hm. Too bad. Well, listen. You wanna go climb a mountain?"

"Are you speaking figuratively or literally?"

"Literally. Me and Debbie're gonna climb Monadnock today and we were wondering if you and Terri'd like to join us. Or you and some other lady. Or just you, if that's how it is."

"Monadnock's not a climb," I said. "It's a stroll up a long hill."

"I know a trail up the back side. I mean, you don't need ropes, but there are some rocks. Okay, so it's not a climb. It's not a stroll, either. Call it a hike."

My head was killing me. The last thing on earth I felt

like doing was climbing a mountain. Which was a very good reason to do it. "Okay," I said. "Climbing Monadnock will give my life some metaphorical significance."

"Whatever that's supposed to mean. Hang on. Debbie wants to say hello."

I took the opportunity to light a cigarette. It did not help my head.

"Hey, Brady?"

Debbie was a junior in high school, a year behind Joey. They'd been together for a year and a half—longer than I'd lasted with Terri, and longer, in fact, than any exclusive relationship I'd managed to sustain with any woman during the decade since Gloria and I were divorced. I wasn't sure how that was significant, but I believed it was. When Joey introduced me to Debbie, she'd called me Mr. Coyne. About the third time the two of them came to my apartment to eat chili and play cards, Debbie had started calling me Brady. I liked it better than Mr. Coyne.

"Hi, kiddo."

"You gonna come with us I hope?"

"Sure."

"Bringing Terri?"

"Nope. She dumped me."

"Aw. That sucks. Want me to fix you up with a friend of mine?"

"What, some high-school junior?"

"No. An older woman." Debbie giggled. "A senior."

"Tempting. But not today, honey. Don't tell Joey, but I'm a wee bit overhung this morning."

"Mountain air'll cure that. Well, see you soon, then. Here's Joe."

"We'll come get you in an hour," he said. "I got the lunches and everything. Don't forget to bring some extra layers and foul-weather gear. This is November. Mountaintops get chilly."

"For Chrissake, son. *You're* the kid, remember?"

"Gets confusing sometimes, doesn't it, Pop?"

"Not to me," I growled.

It wasn't until after I hung up that I wondered how it happened that Debbie and Joey were together at seven on a Saturday morning. And Terri and I weren't.

The sun shone brilliantly in a transparent November sky. The air carried a chilly bite. It was a perfect day to climb a mountain, figuratively as well as literally. Within fifteen minutes the mountain breeze blew my head clear. It felt good to stretch the hamstrings. Joey's trail offered its challenges. It was erratically marked by an occasional splash of white paint on a rock or tree trunk, and we strayed from it a few times. In several places we had to clamber over rocks. Joey went first, then Debbie. He helped her from above and I had the pleasure of boosting her up from underneath. Then they both reached down to haul me up.

When we got to the top Joey unpacked his knapsack and we ate the salami and extra-sharp cheddar sandwiches Debbie had made. Southern New Hampshire lay spread out around us in its muted November colors, and from up there you couldn't see the shopping malls and high-tech office complexes and condominium developments that had invaded the once-rural landscape. Just trees and meadows, hills and distant mountains, meandering country roadways and rivers, the way it had always been. A man or an automobile would have been a speck, impossible to identify. That was the perspective from the mountaintop. From that distance, the details were indistinct. The big picture came into focus.

It was important, I realized, to climb atop a mountain once in a while.

I mentioned these thoughts to Joey and Debbie as we sat there munching our sandwiches. Debbie nodded. Joey told me I should quit with the metaphors.

He was probably right.

We sat up there drinking coffee with our backs against a rock, sheltered from the hard persistent wind, until clouds obliterated the sun. Joey cocked his head at the sky. "We better head back," he said.

Billy, my older boy, is irresponsible and lazy, a dreamer and risk-taker, sometimes a hell-raiser. He'd switched his major about six times at UMass already, and he'd just begun his junior year. Lately, he was talking of quitting altogether and heading west to become a fly-fishing guide, a career I sometimes aspired to myself. He always seemed to have three or four simultaneous girlfriends, who all knew and liked each other and adored Billy.

Joey's the practical one. He got his homework done ahead of time, mowed his mother's lawn—sometimes without even being reminded—and had, as well as I could tell, remained faithful to Debbie for what amounted to a significant chunk of his young postpubescent life. He kept his room reasonably neat and won prizes at science fairs and sent thank-you notes. He always finished what he started.

It was as if I had been divided in half and a whole man was constructed from each contradictory part.

I loved them both equally and without reservation.

So it was Joey who had to remind his father that we ought to get back down the mountain ahead of the storm. Billy would have wanted to experience a November blizzard on a mountaintop.

The snow came quickly on a hard northeast wind, catching us exposed before we had descended into the treeline. It blew at an acute angle, tiny hard pellets of frozen mist. The three of us hastily donned all the layers we had brought with us and plowed downhill. The rocks grew slippery. Joey again went first, and then the two of us helped Debbie down, and once she lost her footing and if I hadn't been gripping her wrist she would have fallen. When we reached the tree line, the trail leveled off a little and the snow became rain, and the three of us turtled our necks into our jackets and slogged through the dripping woods.

The descent seemed to take much longer than the climb. I mentioned this to Joey. He accused me of looking for metaphors again.

We stopped at a coffee shop in Jaffrey for hamburgers and hot tea, and it was after eight in the evening when Joey and Debbie dropped me off. I invited them up, but there was a party in Wellesley that required their presence. I thanked them for inviting me along. They shrugged as if there was nothing strange about a couple of high-school kids wanting a parent to join them for a Saturday outing.

I figured I must have done something right.

I began shucking layers the moment I closed the door to my apartment behind me, and I left a soggy trail of clothes all the way to the bathroom. I got the shower steaming and stood under it until the final vestiges of chill were driven from my bones.

I slipped on a sweatshirt and jeans, made myself a watered-down Jack Daniel's, and it was only when I went into the living room to catch the third period of the Bruins game that I noticed the red light of my answering machine winking at me. Blink-blink, pause. Blink-blink, pause. Two messages.

And that reminded me of Daniel McCloud, and the eight names he had posthumously left for me, and the warnings from Charlie and Horowitz, and Cammie and Oakley, and all the rest of it, and it occurred to me that I had, for one day on Mount Monadnock, not thought about any of it.

I depressed the button on the machine.

"Brady, it's Terri" came the familiar voice. "It's, um, about three Saturday afternoon. I was just—I don't know why I called, actually." She laughed quickly. "Melissa's at Mother's, and it's pretty gloomy outside. I had WBUR on and they were playing Mendelssohn and I was remembering how we . . . Ah, I'm sorry. I guess I just wanted to hear your voice, for some reason. Anyway, hope all's well with you, Brady Coyne." There was a long pause. "Well, 'bye,'" she said softly before the machine clicked.

Then came another voice. "Mr. Coyne? This is Bonnie Coleman. Al's wife, remember? It's around five Saturday. Will you give me a call, please?" She left a number with an 802 area code. Vermont.

I hastily jotted down the number while my machine rewound itself.

Daniel's book, I thought. She'd found Daniel's book.

What was she doing in Vermont?

I lit a cigarette, then pecked out the number she had given me. A man answered. His voice was cultured, elderly, cautious. "Yes?" he said.

"May I speak with Bonnie Coleman please?"

"Who shall I say is calling?"

"My name is Brady Coyne. I'm returning Bonnie's call."

"One moment, sir."

I puffed my Winston and took a sip from my glass of Jack Daniel's. The ice had melted in it.

"Mr. Coyne?"

"Hi, Bonnie. Let's make it Brady."

"Thanks for getting back to me," she said. "I, uh, have some information I'd like to share with you."

"Great. Let's have it."

"It really doesn't lend itself to the telephone. Something I'd like to show you."

"Have you found the book?"

She hesitated. "Not exactly. Look, I'm staying with the Colemans for a while."

"Al's parents?"

"Yes. We're leaning on each other."

"So let's get together, then."

"Good. How's tomorrow?"

"That would work. Where are you?"

"Dorset. Know where it is?"

"Sure. North of Manchester, which is the home of Orvis and the Fly-fishing Museum, on the banks of the fabled and overrated Battenkill River."

"It's a beautiful river."

"It's the trout fishing that's overrated. Where shall we meet?"

She described a coffee shop on the Ethan Allen Highway, known to Vermonters as Historic Route 7A, just north of Manchester Center. We agreed to meet there at noon. I inferred that either she didn't want Al's bereaved parents to see her with another man so soon after their son's death or she wanted to insulate them from the information she had for me.

In either case I found myself intrigued.

Maybe it was a breakthrough. Maybe finally I'd learn something that would connect the dots—the missing manuscript, the list of eight mysterious names, Daniel's murder, as well as Al's, and the strange protective reactions of Charlie and Horowitz to my inquiries.

I tried to conjure up Bonnie Coleman's image from our days in New Haven. I remembered blond hair, a flirtatious smile, long slender legs. But that was more than twenty years ago.

She'd undoubtedly aged. Hadn't we all?

21

I sprawled on the sofa and flicked on the Bruins game. It was tied at two-all midway through the third period and remained that way through the five-minute overtime. Everything was happening between the blue lines. The puck bounced and dribbled from team to team, the players kept trying to knock each other down, and they all seemed less interested in winning than in preventing defeat. Another insight into the human condition. I'd had a productive day at such insights, although any useful applications for them had so far eluded me.

When the game mercifully ended, I clicked off the set and dialed Daniel McCloud's number. Cammie answered with a cautious "Hello?"

"It's Brady."

"Oh, gee. How are you?" I heard Bonnie Raitt in the background.

"I'm fine," I said. "I was just wondering—"

"Brady, can you hold on for a sec? I can't hear you

very well." She put the phone down, and when she came back on a minute or two later I no longer could hear the music. "You still there?"

"I'm here."

"That's better. What's up?"

"I was mainly just wondering if our friend Sergeant Oakley is behaving himself."

"Oh, yes. Since you did whatever you did, I haven't seen him."

"That's good," I said. "Cammie, remember those names?"

"Names?"

"Daniel's photos."

"Oh. Yes, I guess so."

"Have you thought about them?"

"Truthfully, no. I mean, I didn't recognize any of them. They didn't mean anything to me. Just names. You know?"

"Listen. I'm going to read them to you again. I've learned a few things about them. I want you to write them down, think about them some more, maybe rummage around among Daniel's stuff, see if you can come up with anything."

"Do you think this is going to get us anywhere?"

"I don't know. It's all I can think of. Fusco—the state cop—he's apparently given up on the case. Charlie McDevitt and my friend Horowitz are practically ordering me to stop poking around in it. So I can't think of anything else to do."

"You want me to write them down?"

"Yes."

"Hang on. Lemme get a pencil and paper."

A minute or so later she came back on the phone and said, "Okay. Read 'em to me."

I read the eight names to Cammie. I told her what I had learned about each of them. How they all had either died or disappeared. Murder, suicide, accident. Dates. Connections. I went slowly, and several times Cammie asked me to repeat what I had said. When I finished, I said, "And I'm willing to bet that Daniel and Al Coleman—he's the one I sent the manuscript to—that they belong on that list, too."

"Jesus, Brady."

"Any bells chiming for you, Cammie?"

She let out a long breath. "Afraid not."

"You sure?"

She hesitated. "Brady, what are you trying to say?"

"Nothing. I guess I had hoped that with the information that goes along with the names, maybe something would click for you."

"You sound as if you had an idea. A suspicion or something."

"No," I said. "I hoped you did."

"I'm sorry." A pause. "Hey, Brady?"

"Yes?"

"Why don't you come visit me tomorrow? I'll cook something, we can take a walk down by the river."

"It's tempting, Cammie. But I can't. I'm going to meet the widow of Daniel's agent. She might have some information for me."

She laughed softly. "You're incredible."

"Me?"

"You have all these people trying to scare you off the case, and it only makes you poke deeper."

"Somebody's got to."

"And it might as well be you, huh?"

"It might as well," I said.

"Well, will you come see me sometime?"

"Yes. Soon. I promise."

I stared up into the darkness of my bedroom hearing a Tennessee mountain stream in Cammie's soft chuckle and remembering how she looked standing by her easel silhouetted against the floor-to-ceiling glass in her studio, a paintbrush clenched in her mouth, her honey-colored back smooth and bare, her legs long and sleek, how she turned and came to me, the firm slope of her stomach, the high lifting curve of her breasts, and it became a dream, and in the dream I did not grasp her wrists to stop her from undressing me, and when I was completely undressed and she was, too, Cammie had somehow become Terri and I abruptly woke up.

Terri.

I hadn't returned her call.

I drifted back to sleep thinking about it.

I was halfway down the elevator before I realized I was clutching my briefcase. I cursed Julie. Every afternoon she stuffs the thing full of paperwork—my homework, she calls it. She's gotten me into the habit of lugging it back and forth to the office. The habit of opening it every evening has thus far mercifully eluded me. Usually I drop it inside the doorway of my apartment when I get home and pick it up the next morning on my way out.

So now, on a Sunday morning on my way to Vermont, I was carrying my briefcase for my meeting with Bonnie Coleman.

I tossed it onto the backseat of my car and headed out.

The sky was high and pale and the air was brittle on Sunday morning. Calendar winter was still a month away. But in the shaded spots along Route 2, hoarfrost whitened the ground like snow and skim ice glittered in the puddles from Saturday's rain.

I turned north on Interstate 91, then west on Route 9 in Brattleboro, heading across the narrow southernmost width of Vermont. I ascended, then descended the Green Mountain spine, found Route 7A just north of Bennington, and pulled into the peastone lot in front of Dave's Cafe north of Manchester a few minutes before noon.

There were half a dozen cars already parked there. One of them was a burgundy Honda Accord with New York plates.

I went inside. To the left of the lobby was a small bar, apparently closed. To the right lay a dining room. A sign by the entryway said, "Please Seat Yourself." I went in. Some mounted brown trout and deer antlers and framed Currier and Ives prints hung from the knotty pine walls. High-backed booths lined the front and side by the windows.

Tables were scattered across the floor. None of the tables was occupied. Everyone wanted a window view of the highway.

I stood there for a moment. Then I saw a hand and a glimpse of blond hair. I went over and said, "Bonnie?"

She nodded. "I thought that was you. Thanks for coming."

I never would have recognized her on the street, but knowing who she was, I remembered her. Aside from three parallel vertical creases between her eyebrows and a barely noticeable thickening of the flesh on her throat, she still looked pretty much as I remembered her at twenty, although I knew she was at least twice that.

I slid into the booth across from her.

She smiled at me. Her eyes were the same color as the Vermont sky. "I remember you," she said. "You and your friend Charlie. You guys were wild."

I nodded. "We still are."

"I bet. Want some coffee?" She gestured to an earthenware urn and two matching mugs that sat on the table.

"Coffee would be great."

Bonnie poured the two mugs full.

I picked up the one she pushed toward me and sipped. "How are you doing?" I said.

She shrugged. "I'm doing okay. It's hard, but I'm getting there. Al's parents are like big solid slabs of Vermont granite. They've been great. I lean on them and they hold me up. We weren't especially close when—when Al was alive. The kids aren't handling it that well." She shook her head. "It takes time, I guess."

I nodded. "I'm really sorry. Anything I can do . . ."

"Thanks. Time. That's all."

Bonnie talked about New Haven, how she'd met Al when he was a law student and she an undergraduate at Yale, the parties at the place Charlie and I rented on the ocean, how Al started as a State Department attorney, their early married life in Georgetown, how Al became disillusioned, quit, set up a practice in New York and evenually became a literary agent, the famous writers whose passes she had rebuffed.

She waved her hand in the air and smiled. "Hell," she said. "You didn't come all the way up here to listen to my life story." She reached down to the seat beside her and brought up a spiral-bound notebook. She placed it on the table.

"Al's?" I said.

She nodded. "He was pretty haphazard about things. A lousy record keeper. He kept track of his appointments in his head. Otherwise, it was my job. Keeping track of things. Or else we would've gone broke. After he died, I spent more than a month going through all the little scraps of paper he left scattered around, just trying to make sure all the loose ends got tied up before I turned the business over to Keating. Anyway," she said, tapping the notebook with her forefinger, "I found this."

"What's in it?"

"More notes. When he got a manuscript he liked, he'd sometimes want to suggest some changes. He liked to play editor, and he was pretty good at it from what the writers used to tell me. You know, cut a scene here, change the ending there, tighten up a plot line, sharpen a character. He'd usually call up the writer and they'd talk about it. A few of them would even listen to him. Most of them would argue with him. But he kept doing it, because he wanted his books to be good. Anyway, there's a couple of pages in here I wanted to show you, and you'll see why we couldn't really discuss it over the phone."

She picked up the notebook and flipped through it, then turned it around so that it lay open and facing me on the table. She leaned over and twisted her head so that we both could read it.

At the top of the page a black felt-tipped pen had printed the words *SNAKE EATER*, and under that, "BC anony.—Daniel??" I looked up at Bonnie. "The man who wrote the book was called Snake Eater by some of his war buddies," I told her. "This BC would mean me. Brady Coyne. The author was anonymous. His first name was Daniel. I must've mentioned that to Al."

She nodded. "My guess was that this might be your book. This was the only set of notes I couldn't account for."

I glanced through the scratches and scribbles on the page. Much of it was illegible. There were sketches and squiggles, some recognizable such as a bird and a woman's breast and a snake and a palm tree and a man smoking a cigar, others just abstract designs, as if Al's black felt-tip kept doodling randomly as he read. A Freudian could find vast significance in all of it, probably. But I couldn't. Here and there I was able to decipher some of his hieroglyphics, although figuring out what they meant wasn't so easy.

I looked up at Bonnie. "He had awful penmanship."

She smiled. "I think he did it on purpose."

"These are the only ones I can make out." I moved my finger from place to place on the two pages, stopping where the letters made sense to me:

— *ed for gramm & spel*

— *ch w BC re au 2 talk*

— *needs prol*

— *ch w PV* This was underlined three times, and beside it, in green pen, Al had scratched: *Fr 1:00 Rock Cent*

— *PV — Sun* This was the last notation on the second page. It was written in pencil.

I flipped forward through the notebook, but the rest of the pages were blank.

"I know it's not much," said Bonnie.

"Can you make sense of any of it?"

She pointed to *ed for gramm & spel.* "This means edit for grammar and spelling," she said. "Al was a stickler for removing as many objections as possible before he'd show anything to an editor. And this BC must be you again."

"Check with me regarding the author. Al told me he wanted to talk with the author. I told him that Daniel wouldn't do it." I moved my finger. "And here. It must mean he thought it needed a prologue."

Bonnie nodded.

"What about PV?" I said. "It's mentioned twice. Mean anything to you?"

She shook her head. "I thought it might be somebody's initials. An editor or publisher or something. But I know all the publishing people Al dealt with, and there's no house and no editor with the initials PV. I checked our

Rolodex. There are a couple of V names who are writers, but none with the first initial of P. There's also a television guy, someone Al liked to talk to about movie rights. Vance. But it's Jack. There's no PV that I know of."

"Rock Cent?" I said, touching the marks Al had made.

"Rockefeller Center is my guess," said Bonnie. "Al liked to go there to meet with editors, have lunch, watch the girls in little skirts twirl around on their skates, do business." She frowned. "Maybe this refers to some other book, nothing to do with this one. PV could be an author's initials. Or even some kind of abbreviation of a title."

"It could be the pen name Daniel—the author—used," I said.

"But Al didn't know who he was. How could he have an appointment to meet him?"

I shrugged. "Good point."

"And here," she said, twisting her head around so that it was close to mine, "PV again. And Sun must mean Sunday. Another . . ."

Her voice trailed away and she slouched back in the booth. I frowned at her. Tears had welled up in her eyes. "Bonnie?" I said.

She shook her head. "Sorry."

"What is it?"

"Nothing. I'm sorry. Sunday, that's all. Al died—got killed—on a Sunday." She tried to smile. "Oh, I'm doing just fine, I am. Shit." She rummaged in her pocketbook and found a tissue. She dabbed her eyes and blew her nose. "Dammit," she muttered.

"I know this is hard," I said.

She sipped her coffee and made a face. She looked at her watch. "Look," she said, "I've got to get back to the kids."

"Sure. Would you mind if I photocopied these two pages? I'd like to have them to study."

"There's one of those twenty-four-hour places down the road. They've got a copier."

I put a five-dollar bill on the table and we left. I followed Bonnie a mile or so south on 7A. We stopped at a convenience store that doubled as a video rental. I photocopied the two pages from Al Coleman's notebook. It cost me twenty cents.

Outside, Bonnie and I shook hands. "Sorry about the tears," she said.

"You're entitled."

"Thought I was done with all that."

"I don't suppose one ever is."

She smiled, then held out her hand. I took it. "Thanks," she said.

She climbed into her Honda and I watched her drive away.

I slid the two sheets of photocopied paper into my briefcase and headed home. And all the way back to Boston I pondered who—or what—PV could be.

22

I got back to my apartment around four in the afternoon. We were approaching the shortest day of the year, and already the sun had sunk low behind the city's buildings. In my childhood, Sunday afternoons in the wintertime were always my most depressing times, and little has changed since then.

I tucked my car into its reserved spot in the basement garage, retrieved my briefcase from the backseat, and took the elevator up to the sixth floor.

The instant I opened the door I knew something was wrong.

I have an eccentric concept of order, I readily confess. Shoes, T-shirts, bath towels, magazines, fly rods—everything finds its place in my apartment. They usually happen to be places that most people wouldn't consider appropriate. But I know where things are, and if they're not there I know where to look.

I do not, however, keep my private papers scattered

across the living-room rug. I do not keep my desk drawers upside down on the kitchen table or the cushions of my sofa in a heap in the corner or my canned goods and refrigerator contents strewn around the kitchen floor.

My place had been pillaged.

I wandered around the living room, staring at the mess. Whether it had been a thorough job or a hasty one I couldn't tell. Nor could I determine if any papers were missing. My TV was there, and my stereo, and the two Aden Ripley watercolors still hung on the wall. The canned goods and pots and pans had been swept out of the cabinets in the kitchen. The freezer door hung open and melting ice dripped into a big puddle on the floor.

I went back into the living room, shoved the cushions back where they belonged on the sofa, and sat down. I lit a cigarette. My hands, I noticed, were steady.

I remembered Daniel's office the day he was killed. It had been trashed, too.

I smoked the cigarette down to the filter, crushed it out, and stood up. I went into my bedroom. I groped, then found the wall switch. When the light went on, I saw the arrow sticking into my mattress.

It was a mate to the one that had protruded from Daniel McCloud's chest—the same design on the aluminum shaft, the same colored fletching. But instead of slicing up through Daniel's abdomen into his heart, this one had been rammed into my bed—in just about the place my chest would have been had I been sleeping there. It had sliced through the blanket and two layers of sheets and penetrated deep into the mattress.

I have been accused on more than one occasion of not being sensitive or intelligent enough to take a hint.

It's a bum rap. I'm pretty good at understanding hints when I hear them. I just tend to ignore them, which is different.

Anyway, this wasn't a hint.

It was a warning, and a blatant one, and it was the same one that Charlie McDevitt and Horowitz had issued to me.

Only this one was impossible to ignore.

Sticking razor-sharp hunting broadheads into mattresses wasn't Charlie's style, or Horowitz's, either. It was exactly the style of a man who would shove an arrow into a man's abdomen, however.

I sat on the edge of my bed. I gripped the arrow and tried to twist it out. It came reluctantly. "Son of a *bitch*," I muttered. I yanked it from the mattress, then pulled it through the sheets and blanket, and when I got it free big tufts of mattress stuffing clung to the barbed broadhead. It left behind a jagged three-cornered hole in my mattress, just as it would have in my chest.

I carried the arrow out into the kitchen. I poured two fingers of sour mash into a glass, paused, then splashed in some more. I lit another cigarette.

Anger makes me glacially calm and focused. Fear gives me the shakes. I knew I was angry. Getting burglarized made me angry. But I noticed my hands. They were trembling.

I was angry *and* afraid.

A murderer had been in my apartment. I was entitled.

How the hell had he gotten in? It wasn't the most constructive question I could think of. But it was the one that my anger and my fear conspired to raise first.

Part of my hefty monthly rent check goes to paying the security guard who sits in the lobby of the building. He has a bank of closed-circuit television monitors in front of him that he's supposed to watch continually, but that must get a little boring, since he has his own portable television set tuned to more interesting channels. Nobody bothers complaining. Harbor Towers is a quiet building, inhabited mostly by retired old folks who spend the cold half of the year in Florida, plus a few separated or divorced single people like me who appreciate privacy. Nothing much ever happens in my building, and although the guards wear revolvers on their hips, none of the many we've had over the years has ever had an occasion to remove one from its holster.

For a visitor to gain entrance into the building, he must buzz the guard, who will then scrutinize the appropriate closed-circuit monitor and pick up the intercom phone. The visitor will give his name and the number of the unit he is visiting. The guard will ring the unit. The resident will okay his guest, who will then be buzzed in. The visitor will sign into the book, noting his or her name, the number of the unit visited, and the time. All visitors must sign out, too.

Residents, of course, have their own keys.

Most of us who live there park our cars in the basement garage and take the elevator directly up, bypassing the guard. But without our plastic parking card, which we must insert into a slot to make the barrier go up, we can't drive into the garage.

There are four fire doors that open into the building plus a service entrance in the back. They can only be opened from the outside with a passkey. A closed-circuit camera is trained on each of them.

If I wanted to invade a building such as mine, I would walk into the garage, ducking under the barrier and sticking close to the wall so that the closed-circuit camera would miss me. I'd have to take my chances getting onto the elevator, since there's a camera trained on it, too. If I kept my back to the camera, it's unlikely a guard would set off an alarm if he happened to notice me. He'd assume I was a resident even if he were watching that monitor instead of a ball game. Even more foolproof, I'd lurk in the shadows until some residents drove in. Then I'd walk onto the elevator with them. They'd assume I was one of the many residents they had never met. The guard would assume I was their guest. And an hour later my face would be forgotten by all of them.

Of course, if I had a passkey, or was adept at picking locks, I could get in through a fire door and then enter someone's apartment where I could, if that's what turned me on, strew papers around and shove arrows into mattresses.

I called Tony, the weekend guy, through the building intercom.

"Yo," he answered.

"It's Brady Coyne, 6E," I said.

"Hey, Mr. Coyne." Tony was a cheerful guy, a retired

shoe salesman who'd only been on the job for a couple of months. His main responsibility was to be there sitting on his fanny. He liked to watch soap operas and sitcoms, and I figured he barely earned the five bucks or so he was paid per hour.

"What's your shift these days, Tony?" I asked.

"Noon to eight, same as it's been."

"So you've been there since noon today?"

"Yep. Why? Problem?"

"Did anybody come looking for me?"

He hesitated. "You okay, Mr. Coyne?"

"I'm fine."

"You sound a little—I don't know—shaky."

"I'm okay. Was there anybody for me?"

"Um. Hm. Nope. Nobody. Expecting someone?"

"No, not really," I said. "Did anybody come looking for anybody who wasn't home? Or did you notice anything suspicious at all today?"

"Nah. Quiet day. Sunday, you know?"

"Any deliveries?"

"Nope. Sunday. You sure you're okay?"

"Yes, dammit." I took a breath. "I'm sorry, Tony. Listen, did you catch anything from the garage?"

"Whaddya mean?"

"I don't know. I'm just wondering if you saw anyone you didn't recognize today, someone who might've come around and then left, or buzzed me but found me out or something."

"Jeez, no, Mr. Coyne. Nothin' like that. Quiet. It's Sunday."

"Who was on before you?"

"That was Lyle. He had four to noon."

"Take a look in the book, see what's there after nine this morning."

"Like what?"

"Guests. Anybody who might've signed in."

"Okay. Hang on." There was a minute or two of silence, then Tony said, "Nothin' here, Mr. Coyne. Sunday morning, people go out. No guests at all. You know, half the tenants are away anyhow."

"Sure. Did Lyle make any notations?"

"Huh? What kind of notations?"

"I don't know. That he saw anything unusual."

"I guess he would've called in an alarm if he did, huh? That's what we're supposed to do. Anything at all, just buzz the police. He would've noted it if he'd done that. Nothing here. Quiet day. Sunday."

"Right," I said. "Sunday. Listen, has anybody reported losing their keys?"

"Keys?"

"House keys."

"Jeez, no. I heard nothing like that from anybody."

"Okay." I hesitated. "Well, thanks anyway, Tony. If you think of something, give me a buzz, will you?"

"Sure. You bet. Hey, Mr. Coyne. Really. Somethin' wrong?"

"No. No problem. Thanks."

"You bet."

I took my drink and my souvenir hunting arrow to the glass sliders and stared out into the November night. I fondled the arrow and sipped my drink. My hands were no longer trembling. All I saw outside was darkness. I went back to the phone and dialed Charlie's number at home. When he answered, I said, "How'd you feel if someone got a key to your place, sauntered in, trashed it, and stuck an arrow into your bed?"

"What the hell are you talking about?"

"When I got home this afternoon I found the place turned upside down. There was an arrow up to its hilt in my mattress. It looks identical to the one that was sticking in Daniel. I've been trying to sort out my feelings. Anger and fear, mingled together. Lots of fear, I think."

"For Chrissake, Brady—"

"I'm sorry," I said quickly. I took a deep breath. "I'm not accusing you of anything."

"It kinda sounded like it."

"Well, I'm not. I just need to talk to somebody. Look. This thing has freaked me out, Charlie."

"An arrow sticking into your bed? I don't blame you."

"I was away most of the day. When I got back it was there. Right where I would've been if I'd been asleep."

"A warning, you figure, huh?"

"Of course. What else? The sonofabitch was *here*. First you warned me, then Horowitz warned me, now this."

"Horowitz? The state cop?"

"Yes. He told me what you told me."

"About Daniel?"

"Yes."

"To back off?"

"Yes. In the strongest possible terms. Like you did."

"Well, you don't think Horowitz broke into your place, trashed it, and jammed some arrow into your bed, do you?"

"Of course not."

"Or me?"

"Shit, no, Charlie. I didn't intend that at all. I just don't know what to think. I know what I'm *supposed* to think. I'm supposed to think I better stop trying to figure out who killed Daniel."

"You should, you know."

"Yeah, well, maybe you're right."

"Well, good. It's about time you got some sense." Charlie let out a long breath. "Did they take anything?"

"I don't know. I don't think so. Maybe it was all just to make an impression. Rip up the place, stick an arrow into the bed where I could've been. Just a message."

"A pretty blatant message, at that," he said.

"Charlie, I don't know what to do. Jesus . . ."

"You could have been lying in that bed, Brady."

"Don't think for one minute that hasn't occurred to me."

"Next time, then."

"I know. Thanks for the sympathy."

"That why you called? For sympathy?"

"I don't know why I called. You're acting weird lately."

"*Me?* Me weird? Check the mirror, Coyne."

"I did. I saw this guy who just had the wee-wee scared out of him."

"That's better than seeing someone with an arrow in him."

"He's also pretty mad, this guy in the mirror," I said.

"Listen to the scared part, Brady. That's the part that makes sense."

"I know."

"Look," he said. "I don't know anything about this, and yes, I'm concerned. I'm frightened, too, okay? I don't want to lose you, buddy, and I'm glad you called me. But exactly what do you want?"

I laughed quickly. "I don't know. Not advice, because you already gave me that, and it's sounding more and more sensible all the time. Not sympathy, because that's useless. Your friendship doesn't need confirming. Maybe I hoped you'd have some insights, but I suppose I didn't really think you would. I guess I just wanted to vent."

"Vent away."

"I already did."

"Lemme think about it," said Charlie.

"Okay."

"I'm a little confused myself," he said.

"Those names disappearing from your computer's memory."

"Yeah. That's strange." He hesitated, then said, "Hey, Brady?"

"What?"

"You called the cops, didn't you?"

"Why?"

"Jesus! To tell them about the burglary, the arrow in your bed."

"And what would the cops do?"

Charlie hesitated; then he chuckled. "They'll ask you

if anybody is hurt. You'll say no. And about four hours later they'll arrive, glance around, ask if anything's missing, drop some cigar ashes onto your carpet, and you'll end up feeling as if you're the criminal. That's if they show up at all."

"Exactly. I talked to the security guy. That's as much as the cops would do. He didn't know anything."

"You should still call them. Report the crime. Be a good citizen."

"Yeah, well, I probably won't."

"Listen," he said.

"I know what you're going to say."

"I'm gonna say it anyway. Please. Stop. Cease and desist. Trust me on this."

"I trust you, Charlie."

"So what're you gonna do?"

"I don't know. Sleep on the sofa, I guess."

And after I cleaned up my apartment and made sure the chain was secured and the deadbolt thrown, that's what I did, although I didn't do much actual sleeping. Mostly I stared up into the darkness. I keep a .38 in the safe in my office. I decided to remove it the next day and bring it home with me.

Otherwise, I didn't come up with any helpful ideas.

I dozed off, then abruptly awoke. It could have been ten minutes later. Or several hours. I didn't check the time. I thought I had heard something. I lay there in the darkness, trying not to move. I felt a vise around my chest. My breaths came quickly. I darted my eyes around the shadowy corners of my living room. I heard nothing, saw nothing.

My heart was tripping along like a snare drum.

I switched on the lights and padded barefoot through all my rooms, wishing I had my .38 in my hand.

Nobody was there but me.

I retrieved my briefcase from the floor by the door and opened it. I found the envelope with the photos and index cards, and the printout Charlie had given me, and the two photocopied pages from Al Coleman's notebook. I brought them to the sofa and looked at them. I didn't know what I expected to find. I picked up the photos and fanned them out like a poker hand. I studied the six black-and-white faces as if they might speak to me. Six ordinary-looking American men gazed blankly back at me. They said nothing. I put them down and took up the index cards. William Johnson. Carmine Repucci. Two minor-league crooks who ended up violently murdered, the way most of them do. No faces. Just two names.

After a while I became sleepy. Those eight names and a faceless man with an arrow in his hand all swirled through my brain as I drifted off for the second time that night, and when I awakened the sun was streaming into my living room, and if I'd had dreams of arrows being rammed into me, I'd blissfully forgotten them.

23

I dialed Cammie's number standing up while sipping my second cup of coffee, and Daniel's voice startled me for an instant before I realized it was his answering machine.

"I'm not here. Say who you are and I'll get back to you" was all he said.

After the beep, I said, "You should get the message on the machine changed, Cammie. It's Brady. About nine Monday morning. Please call me at the office right away." I left the number, hung up, grabbed my jacket, and headed out.

Julie was on the phone and Rita Nathanson was waiting for me. I smiled at both of them, and neither smiled back. Rita's appointment was at nine. I was half an hour late.

"Sorry I'm late," I said. "Come on in, Rita."

Rita's ex-husband had stopped sending child-support checks from Boise, Idaho, where he had retreated upon their separation. When she called me the previous week, I told her that it would take a while but I'd handle it. She insisted on a meeting. I knew what she wanted. She wanted to cuss the bastard out to a sympathetic ear. That's one of the things I offer my clients. A sympathetic ear. Maybe not a sympathetic soul, but at least an ear.

It's billable time, and a good deal for all concerned. I charge a little less for an hour of ear-lending than do most of my psychoanalyst friends. When my clients run out of useful cusses, I'm generally able to supplement their repertoire.

For that half hour with Rita, I almost forgot Daniel and Al Coleman and my ransacked apartment and that arrow sticking out of my mattress.

After Rita left, Julie stormed my portal. She was intolerant of my haphazard office hours, especially when we had a busy week facing us. I pretended to be properly chagrined, and finally I made her smile. Then she sat down and laid out the week's schedule of appointments, conferences, and court appearances for me. I murmured during her pauses, and after a few minutes, she stopped and said, "Brady, what's eating you?"

I shook my head. "It's too complicated to explain. I'm okay."

"You're . . . different. This isn't woman problems. Something wrong with one of the boys?"

"No. It's nothing. Go ahead."

She shrugged and finished giving me my instructions. I paid closer attention. And after she left, I tried to focus on all the projects she had left with me. It was slow going.

Cammie called a little before noon. When Julie put her through, I said, "Hi, Cammie."

"Gee, hi. I just came up from the studio and saw the machine blinking. I gotta get a phone down there, I guess. What's up?"

"We need to talk."

"Boy, sounds ominous."

I tried to laugh. "Not ominous. Some things have happened, but mainly I want you to look at these photos. I've given you the names, but you haven't seen the faces." I hesitated. "And I've got some thoughts I want to share with you."

"Sure. Okay. When?"

"The sooner the better. How's tonight?"

"Tonight's good. What time?"

"I'll come right from the office. I'll try to get away by five. I can hit the pike and be there in two hours. Say seven?"

"I'll cook something for us, then."

"Don't do anything special." I paused. "See if Brian and Roscoe and Vinnie can be there, too. They can help. We can all put our heads together."

"Sure. Okay."

I failed to take into account five o'clock outbound traffic on the Mass Pike, and it was after seven-thirty when I pulled up in front of Daniel's house in Wilson Falls.

I grabbed my briefcase from the backseat, climbed the front steps, and rang the bell. Cammie pulled the door open. She was wearing a short black skirt over black tights and a bulky orange sweater and a tentative smile.

She grabbed my hand and led me to the living room. Brian Sweeney was sitting on the sofa. He had a drink in his hand and the stub of a cigar in his mouth. He stood up and we shook hands.

"How ya been?" he said.

"I'm okay. You?"

He shrugged.

"Drink?" said Cammie.

"Sure."

"Bourbon, right?"

I nodded. I sat on the sofa beside Sweeney while Cammie went into the kitchen. "Are Roscoe and Vinnie coming?" I said.

"I guess not," he said. "Cammie said she tried to call them. Nobody home."

Cammie came back with my drink. "I tried several times," she said. "I guess they're away. If you want, I'll try again after we eat."

"Good idea," I said.

"I'm going to broil some fish," she said. "It'll take about fifteen minutes. Everything else is ready. I thought we could have a drink first."

"Fine," I said.

Cammie looked at me over the rim of her glass. "Do you want to talk now or later, Brady?"

"Later, I think. Maybe Roscoe and Vinnie can make it."

"All right."

I told Cammie and Sweeney about climbing Mount Monadnock with my son and his girlfriend, and all of us carefully avoided mentioning Daniel or the circumstances of his death or Sergeant Oakley or anything unpleasant. When we finished our drinks Cammie got up and brought me and Sweeney refills then she went into the kitchen.

"You got it figured out, Brady?" said Sweeney.

"No," I said. "I've got some new questions, that's all. And I've got these photos I wanted you guys to see."

"What kind of questions?"

"Let's hold it till we've eaten. I want Cammie in on it, too."

The broiled swordfish was garnished with sprigs of fresh parsley. The little golf ball red-skinned potatoes had been boiled, then drenched in butter. Green beans and slivered almonds, avocado salad, a smooth white wine.

Sweeney and I cleared the dishes from the table. Cammie tried Roscoe and Vinnie again, and again got no answer.

We took coffee back into the living room. Cammie and Brian sat beside each other on the sofa. I took the chair across from them. I had my briefcase on my lap.

"Okay, Brady," said Cammie. "Now. What's up?"

I reached into my briefcase and took out the envelope with the photos in it. I laid them on the coffee table so Cammie and Brian could see them.

"These are what you found in Daniel's papers, huh?" said Sweeney.

"Yes. Recognize any of them?"

He picked them up one by one, looked at them closely, turned each of them over to read the name and address, then handed them to Cammie, who did the same thing. When they were both done they looked at me.

"Nothing," said Brian.

"Me, neither," said Cammie. She frowned at me. "You said there were eight photos . . ."

"Six photos. There were two index cards with names and addresses on them in with the photos. The names were William Johnson and Carmine Repucci."

Cammie and Brian both shrugged.

I leaned across the coffee table and touched Cammie's hand. "What was Boomer's name?" I said.

She frowned. "Boomer?" She shook her head. "I don't know. Everybody called him Boomer."

"When you were . . . with him, with Boomer—you never heard the names William Johnson or Carmine Repucci, then?"

"No. I—" Her hand went to her mouth and her eyes widened.

"What is it?"

"Pooch," she whispered.

"Huh?"

"Pooch. Repucci." She turned to Brian. "Those two names . . ."

"You knew Repucci?" I said.

She turned back to face me. "If Pooch was Repucci, then Boomer was . . ."

"William Johnson," I finished for her.

"I don't get it," said Brian.

"They were both murdered," I said. "I think Daniel killed them both."

Cammie stared at me for a minute, then nodded. "Yes," she said. "Yes, that fits."

"Tell me," I said.

Her dark eyes stared into mine for a moment. Then she sighed and nodded. "Okay. There's not much to tell. Brian's heard most of it. Boomer picked me up one night in Springfield. I was just at rock bottom, Brady. I didn't know who I was, where I came from, what I was doing, how I got there. I was in a bar, trying to hustle coke money. He took me home, gave me a couple of lines, made love to me. Told me he loved me, he wanted to take care of me. It's what I thought I needed. I had lost my soul. He filled in the empty place. He *became* my soul, do you see? And he had a supply. He gave me everything I needed. After a while he put me out on the streets. I had to work for it. Pooch was a friend of his, his supplier, I think. I was frightened of Pooch. I thought I loved Boomer. But what did I know? I was a junkie. A cokehead. I didn't know either of their real names. They just called each other 'Boomer' and 'Pooch.' I didn't care what their names were. Anyway, Daniel came along. He found me on the street and brought me here and straightened me out. Then *he* became my soul. It was different. He *did* love me. I lived in fear of Boomer for years. He had always made it clear that if I tried to get away he'd cut my face. But I never saw him. It was several years later when I saw Pooch. After Daniel saved me, after I got off the coke, after I started painting and loving Daniel, after I had finally stopped being afraid of Boomer. I saw Pooch sitting in a car in the parking lot outside the Star Market in Wilson Falls. Parked right next to my car. I was petrified. I dropped my groceries on the ground and just got out of there. I had to get back to Daniel. Pooch, he—he just smiled at me. Sitting there in his car smiling at me through the tinted window, and I thought if I just get back to Daniel everything will be okay."

"Did Repucci ever bother you after that?"

"No. I never saw him again."

"Because Daniel killed him."

She shrugged, then nodded. "I guess so. It makes sense now." She stared at me for a moment. "Daniel killed them for me. Boomer and Pooch . . . I never knew their real names."

"So if he killed those two," said Sweeney. "You think . . . ?"

I nodded. "It fits."

Cammie shook her head. "You think he killed those others, too?" She frowned. "But why? Who were they, anyway? Jesus, Brady. Who killed Daniel, then?"

"At first I thought it was in the book," I said. "It was a book about those eight men in Daniel's insurance file. Somebody killed them, and in the book Daniel named the killer, so that man killed Daniel, too, and ransacked his office looking for the book. The book was the evidence. And the same man killed Al Coleman, because he had the book, and he'd read it, so he knew. That's what I thought at first. Then it occurred to me that William Johnson was your Boomer. His profile fit what you told me about him. He and Repucci were together in prison, both ended up in Springfield, where Daniel found you. You and Daniel both had good reason to kill them. Truthfully, my first thought was that you did it. But that would mean you'd killed all eight of them, and Daniel and Al Coleman, too, and I didn't believe that. That left Daniel. Now, if Daniel himself was the killer of Johnson and Repucci and the other six, these here"—I touched the six photographs on the coffee table—"then we've got another killer to think about. Somebody who, for some reason, didn't want Daniel to publish his confession. So this other person killed Daniel and he killed Al to make sure the secret in that book would never get out."

Cammie was frowning at me. "What secret?" she said. "Who'd want to keep it a secret besides Daniel?"

"I'm not sure."

"I'm confused," said Sweeney.

I nodded. "It's complicated. I need your help in sorting it out."

The two of them slumped back on the sofa. "Wow," whispered Cammie.

"Wow is right," said Sweeney. "Listen, do you want more coffee?"

"Sure," I said.

Cammie started to get up, but Sweeney touched her arm. "Sit tight," he said. "I'll get it." He stood up and went to the kitchen.

"I wish Roscoe and Vinnie were here," said Cammie. "Daniel was closer to Brian, but he saw Roscoe and Vinnie about every day. They might be able to help."

"We'll catch up to them," I said.

Cammie reached over and put her hand on my arm. "Something's bothering you, Brady."

I shrugged and nodded.

"What is it?"

"I had an uninvited visitor yesterday."

"A what?"

"I was away for most of the day. When I got back, my place had been ransacked. And I found an arrow sticking into my mattress."

"An arrow?"

"Yes. The mate to the one that killed Daniel."

Her fingernails dug into my arm. "Oh, God. Who—?"

Sweeney came back into the room. At first I didn't notice it. Then he raised his arm and I saw what he was holding. It wasn't a coffeepot. It was an autoloading shotgun with the barrel cut back to about twelve inches. He waved it at me. "Whyn't you sit over there beside her," he said.

"I'll be damned," I said.

"Just do it, Brady."

I got up and sat beside Cammie. Sweeney took the chair.

Cammie was staring at him. "Brian, what are you . . . ?"

"It was him," I said to her. "He killed Daniel."

"How . . . ?"

"When you think about it, it's simple," I said. "Who else could get that close to Daniel, catch him with his guard down? Either Roscoe or Vinnie, or both of them together. Or Brian."

She frowned at me, then turned to Sweeney. "Brian?" she whispered.

"It's a long story," he said. "You don't need to know."

She stared hard at him. "If I'd known this . . ."

Sweeney shrugged. "Better that you didn't know."

"You son of a bitch," she whispered.

"Listen," he said. "Both of you. Let me tell you a story. Our team was in the jungle, and some of the snake eaters were scouting a village, and the rest of us were hiding by an old cart path, and along came a couple of dogs, and behind them was this old grandmother and two little boys. The dogs sniffed us out where we were hiding, and they started yapping and the grandmother and the kids saw us, so Daniel says we've gotta kill them all or they'll go back and there'll be VC all over the place. So—"

"I don't want to hear this," said Cammie quickly.

Sweeney held up the hand that wasn't holding the shotgun. "Listen to the story, darlin'," he said. "You'll learn something. So I killed them. Daniel ordered me to do it. I told him I couldn't do it, and he took out his forty-five and pressed it against my ear and ordered me to do it. So I did. I was nineteen years old. I got up and went to those people and gave them candy bars and cut their throats. Then I killed the dogs, too." Sweeney shrugged. "Something like that changes a man."

"So you hated him for that," she said.

"Huh?" he said.

"You hated Daniel. Enough to kill him."

He shrugged and smiled at both of us, and when he did he reminded me of Daniel, the way he used to shrug, with a quick roll of his eyes and a twitch of his shoulders. "He made me see a part of myself I didn't like," he said. "I couldn't forgive him for that. But hate?" He frowned, weighing the accuracy of the word. Then he shook his head. "No. I loved him. I owe him my life. We all do. He was our leader. Our father. He made us do things that we didn't want to do. But we understood. We had to do them to survive. He made us grow up. He showed us things in ourselves that we didn't know were there, that we didn't want to know were there. Oh, some of the men hated him, I know. But they were too afraid of him to admit it. And even they loved him, too. Like you love a father you also fear and think you hate."

"But you killed him," I said.

He shrugged. "Daniel taught me how. He taught me that I could."

"Tell me about Al Coleman," I said.

"Nothing to tell. Something that had to be done."

"Because he had the book."

"He had the book. And he knew."

"About you?"

"No," said Sweeney. "About Daniel."

24

Sweeney picked up my briefcase and set it on the coffee table. "What other goodies you got in here?"

I reached for it. "I'll show you."

"That's okay." He grinned. "You just relax."

He opened the briefcase and reached in. He removed the computer printouts that Charlie had given me, and the photocopied pages from Al's notebook. He spread them out on the coffee table and glanced at them without entirely taking his attention from me and Cammie sitting across from him.

"You've been busy," he said.

I shrugged.

He reached into the briefcase again. His hand came out with my .38 in it. "My, my," he said. He held it up and peered at it. "All loaded and everything." He squinted at me. "You knew what was going to happen tonight, huh?"

"No," I said. "I didn't know what was going to happen. I just figured something would. I didn't know whether it would be you or Roscoe or Vinnie or even Cammie. Or maybe none of you. Maybe I was way off base." I shrugged. "Somebody broke into my apartment yesterday. I kind of figured whoever it was would make it a point to be here tonight. Whoever it was really wanted these photographs."

Sweeney held the shotgun steady with his right hand. It was pointing at my chest. With his left hand he put the photos and papers and my .38 back into the briefcase. He snapped it shut and dropped it onto the floor beside him. "It's getting stuffy in here," he said. "Let's go outside, get some fresh air."

Cammie frowned, then said, "I can open a window."

"He's not really making a suggestion," I said.

She looked at me and nodded. She started to stand up.

"Wait," said Sweeney. "Put your hands behind your necks. Both of you."

"Jesus," said Cammie.

I laced my fingers behind my neck. "Do it," I said to her.

She did. Then we both stood up. Sweeney stood, too. "Okay," he said. "Let's go get some air."

We went out onto the deck. Sweeney stayed about five paces behind us with his ugly sawed-off autoloading shotgun leveled on us at his waist. When we descended the steps onto the lawn, he said, "Okay. Why don't you put your arms around each other? Like you were lovers out for a stroll."

"Brian," began Cammie. But she stopped. I put my arm across her back and rested my hand on her hip. I felt her shiver against the chill November air. Her arm went around my waist. That way, it would be impossible for either of us to make a sudden move at Sweeney.

He directed us along a path through the woods. The sky was clear and bright with the moon, and we had no problem following the path. Through the trees off to our left I could see moonlight glimmer on the river, and I recognized the place where Daniel and I had fished. But we didn't angle toward the river there. We kept moving, and the path narrowed so that Cammie and I had to fend off branches as we walked hip to hip.

Suddenly Sweeney whispered, "Stop!"

We stopped, and Cammie said, "What—?"

"Shut up!" he hissed.

We stood there, not moving. I moved my hand up and down Cammie's side, hoping to comfort her, and I could feel the tenseness in her muscles. She pressed her arm against my hand and held it tight against her.

I tried to hear what Sweeney had heard. A soft breeze hissed through the trees and made crinkly noises among the brittle oak leaves that still clung stubbornly to their branches. A dog barked far across the river.

Otherwise I heard nothing.

After a minute or two, Sweeney said, "Okay. Let's go."

We continued to push through the forest. Cammie and I walked arm-in-arm. We used our free outside forearms to deflect the brush that grew close to the path. Sweeney remained five or six steps behind us, far enough back so that the saplings would not whip against him after we passed, but close enough to hear us if Cammie and I tried to whisper and certainly close enough to spray both of us easily with buckshot if we tried a sudden move.

Sweeney, I realized, had done this before. He'd crept along narrow jungle paths at night with all his senses raw and alert. He'd probably moved prisoners who he knew would kill him if they could. And none of them ever had. He'd been trained to kill, and he had killed. He'd learned how to survive, and he'd done it. He'd killed and survived as a profession. Even after he left the jungles of Indochina.

He'd killed Daniel. And I had cried when the bagpipes played "Going Home" and Daniel's ashes sifted through Brian Sweeney's fingers, and partly, at least, I had cried because I could see how he had loved the man he called the Snake Eater.

He would kill me and Cammie, too. It was easy for him. After he'd killed a Vietnamese grandmother and two little peasant boys and their dogs, he had learned he could kill anybody.

After we'd been walking for about fifteen minutes, Sweeney said, "Go left here."

We pushed through the undergrowth where there was no path, descended a long slope, and found ourselves on the banks of the Connecticut. The river was broad and slow-moving there. Far across the way I could see a few orange pinpricks of light, and I imagined people in their homes watching television, brushing their teeth, making love in their bedrooms.

Cammie and I stood there on the half-frozen mud beside the water, still holding each other by the waist. The slow eddying currents lapped softly against the rocks. Sweeney stood behind us.

"Okay," I said. "Now what?"

"Wade in."

"Are you—?"

"Do it," he said quietly.

"Can I ask a question first?" I said.

"No."

"But there's a couple things—"

"No," he said. "Wade in."

"This is pretty good," I said. "You kill us in the water, and we float downstream for a while, and the police will never be able to figure out where we were shot, and after our bodies have been in the cold water for a while they'll have a helluva time trying to determine the time of our death, and by the time they find our bodies you'll be back in Vermont, and if anyone thinks to question you, you'll swear that's where you've been right along, and nobody will be able to say different."

"Just walk into the water," said Sweeney. "Slowly."

"Come on," I said to Cammie, urging her with my hand against the side of her waist.

We stepped in. For just an instant I felt nothing. Then the frigid water penetrated my shoes and my feet instantly went numb. I could feel the slow currents tug at my pantlegs. With my arm around her waist I helped Cammie keep beside me. I patted her hip, trying to comfort her, to tell her that it was okay, that I had a plan. When we had waded in up to our waists I would signal her with my fingers, alerting her, then I'd yell, "Now!" and I'd push her away from me and dive quickly to the side in the opposite direction from her, and maybe Sweeney would choose to shoot at me instead of her, and maybe he'd even panic and hesitate too long and miss both of us, and we could swim a long way under water, out toward the middle of the river beyond the short range of Sweeney's sawed-off shotgun. We could swim and float far downriver. It was a chance. We could get away. One of us might, anyway. Cammie, probably. It would be me he'd go for first. If I could dive deep enough quickly enough, the pellets would not penetrate the water with enough force to kill me.

When we were in up to our knees, Sweeney said, "Okay. Stop there."

Too shallow, I thought. He knew what I'd been thinking. If we tried to dive in knee-deep water, he'd get one of us at least.

"Turn around."

Cammie and I had to release each other to turn to face him.

He stood about ten feet from us, only a few feet from the brushy banks of the river. The water came to his ankles. He was holding that wicked weapon in his right hand. The stubby barrel was braced across his left forearm. It didn't waver. The black hole of the bore stared at my chest. He'd go for me first. Cammie might still have a chance.

I put my arm around Cammie's back. She let her arms dangle at her sides.

"I got nothing against you," Sweeney said. "Either of you."

"Why don't you just do me," I said. "No purpose in killing her. She didn't do anything. She doesn't know anything."

Sweeney laughed softly. "Neither do you," he said.

Keep him talking, I thought. As long as he's talking to us, he won't shoot us.

"You're right," I said. "I don't understand any of it. So

Daniel killed those guys. So what? What's it to you? You killed Daniel? Why? It makes no sense."

"It doesn't have to make sense to you."

"Let her go, Brian."

"I wish I could. But—"

The gunshot exploded suddenly, and I reacted to it like a sprinter to the starter's gun. I shoved Cammie away from me and dived sideways, and I didn't feel anything except the frigid water, a quick paralysis in my chest, and I pushed under water as hard and as deep as I could. I heard another explosion, muffled down there with my ears in the water, and at first I was exhilarated that he had missed me, and then I realized that he must have gone for her first, and part of my mind tried to tell me to turn back, to try to help her, to go for Sweeney. But I kept swimming toward the middle of the river, as deep under water as I could go. There was nothing I could do for Cammie. If he'd missed her somehow, she'd make it. If he got her, there was no reason to go back to Sweeney except to let him kill me, too.

I stayed under until I grew faint and my lungs burned. I forced myself to surface slowly. I rolled over so that my face pointed up, and I allowed just my nose and mouth to break through the skin of the water. I gasped deeply for air, and my breath sounded harsh in my ears. I found that my toes reached bottom. Cautiously I stood with just the top half of my head out of water and turned toward the shore.

A flashlight was playing across the water's surface, moving toward me. Quickly I ducked under. I could see it pass over my head. After it swung by, I lifted up again.

I heard Sweeney call this time. "It's all right," he was

calling, in a voice that wasn't his own. "He's dead. You can come in."

I'm not dead, I thought. Don't go to him, Cammie. It's not all right.

"Come on in here," he yelled. "You're gonna freeze."

Then I recognized the voice. It wasn't Sweeney.

It was Oakley.

25

I stood there up to my ears in the Connecticut River, and I found that the adrenaline that had flooded through me was gone. I began to shake uncontrollably against the frigid water, and maybe in a delayed reaction against the fear, too.

Oakley was talking conversationally from the bank of the river, and his voice carried clearly across the river's surface. "He's dead, Miss Russell. Mr. Coyne, it's okay. You can come back. I'm not going to hurt you. Come on. You'll freeze out there."

His flashlight continued to move across the water, and when it approached me I instinctively ducked under until it had passed. Then I bobbed up again.

Oakley said, "I'm a policeman. You folks are safe now. Come in. You've got to get warm."

From somewhere off to my left came Cammie's voice. "Brady? Are you all right?"

"I'm fine," I said. "Let's go in."

The flashlight swung to me, went past, stopped, came back. It held me in its glare, and for a moment I thought Oakley intended to shoot me after all. "Move the light," I said.

It swung away, and I watched it find Cammie. She was wading to shore thirty or forty yards downriver from me.

When I got to shore Cammie was huddled inside a bulky black-and-red checked wool jacket that I assumed was Oakley's, and Oakley was standing there, holding the flashlight pointed down so that its beam reflected off the water and lit up the area. He was wearing a shoulder holster over his sweater. The handle of a revolver protruded from it.

Brian Sweeney lay facedown in six inches of water a few feet from the muddy bank of the river.

"Miss Russell, Mr. Coyne, you folks better get back to the house and find some dry clothes or you'll catch pneumonia. Call the station for me and tell them that I'll be here with the body. Okay?"

"Okay," I said.

"Wait there until they come, then maybe one of you can bring them here. We'll talk all about it later."

I put my arm around Cammie's shoulders and we trudged back through the woods to Daniel's house. We walked as fast as we could in our wet clothes, and as long as we were moving and the blood was circulating I didn't feel the chill.

As soon as we got into the living room we stripped off our clothes. Cammie padded naked to the bathroom and came back with a pair of big bath towels. We rubbed each other's bodies with them, and after a minute or two of that Cammie put her arms around me and pressed herself against me, and I held her while she sobbed.

After a while I felt her body relax. She tilted up and kissed my jaw. "I'll find some clothes for you," she said.

I wrapped the towel around my waist and went to the phone. I dialed 911 and told them to come to Daniel's house, that Sergeant Oakley was here with a dead body.

When Cammie came back, she was wearing jeans and a sweatshirt and had a bundle of clothes in her arms. Daniel's sweatshirt fit fine except the arms were too short. His pants were loose at my waist and the cuffs came halfway up my calves.

We went into the kitchen. Cammie poured some Wild Turkey into a pair of glasses. We stood there leaning against the counter with our own thoughts, not talking, just sipping and staring out into the night until the police arrived behind the wailing of their sirens.

Cammie and I went out onto the front porch to meet them. There were four or five cars and an ambulance. Police Chief Francis Padula stepped from the passenger side of a squad car and came to the steps. "Where is he?" he said.

"I'll show you," I said.

I led a parade through the woods to the river where Oakley was waiting with Sweeney's body. Besides the chief there were two uniformed policemen, one detective, two EMTs, a photographer, and a medical examiner. After I showed them to the place, one of the uniformed cops walked me back to the house. Cammie was seated on the sofa in the living room. A detective had pulled up a chair in front of her, and they were talking quietly. They looked up when the cop and I entered. Cammie tried to smile at me and failed. The detective said, "Take him into the other room." Then they resumed their conversation.

The cop and I went out into the kitchen. I poured a little more bourbon into my glass and sat with it at the table. The cop remained standing. He was guarding me. I ignored him.

After a while the detective came in and nodded at the policeman, who left, presumably to go stand watch over Cammie.

The detective sat across from me. "Nichols," he said, and he held his hand to me. I shook it.

"Tell me," he said.

"It's much too complicated to try to tell more than once."

"Let's start with an easy one. Who's the dead guy?"

"His name is Brian Sweeney. He was a friend of Cammie Russell's."

"Oakley killed him?"

"Yes."

"You see it?"

"Not exactly."

"Explain."

"Look," I said. "Really. Am I going to have to do this again?"

"Probably."

"For the DA?"

"Among others. Yes."

"I don't understand much of it," I said.

"Just what you know, Mr. Coyne. What you saw. I just want you to tell me what happened tonight. Your speculations you can hang on to for now. Okay?"

"Okay." So I told Detective Nichols that I had come to visit Cammie and Sweeney, that she had cooked dinner for us, and that afterward, while we were in the living room, Sweeney had gone into another room and come back with his gun. He forced us to walk down to the river and then wade in, and I assumed he was going to shoot us, but Oakley got him first.

I could see the questions in Nichols's face. But he didn't ask them. "Okay" was all he said.

When Chief Padula came back an hour or so later, I told him the same story, and he just said we'd have to make a deposition the next morning, and I realized that the Wilson Falls police were mainly concerned with the fact that one of their officers had killed a man, and they needed to know whether it was justifiable.

All the other questions would be asked eventually, I assumed.

The cars pulled away one by one, as the various jobs were completed. Finally the only ones left were Padula and Oakley.

"If you wouldn't mind putting on some coffee, Miss," said the chief, "Richard and I would like to talk to you."

Cammie eyed Oakley warily, then went into the kitchen. The rest of us followed her. She put together the coffee, and all four of us sat at the table listening to the pot burble. We didn't talk. When the coffee was ready, Cammie got up and poured four mugs full.

Oakley looked at Cammie. "Francis says I gotta tell you this. That I owe it to you."

She shrugged, avoiding his eyes.

Oakley glanced at Padula, who nodded quickly to him.

"I guess you think I've been harassing you," said Oakley. "That I've been out to get you or something." He paused, staring at Cammie, as if he wanted her to say something. When she didn't look up at him, he said, "Okay. Maybe I owe you an apology. So I'm sorry. I am. I never meant it that way. But I want you to understand."

She glanced up at him, then looked back down into her coffee.

"I had—I have a daughter," said Oakley. "About your age. What're you, twenty-four, twenty-five?"

"Twenty-nine," mumbled Cammie.

He nodded quickly. "Janie's her name. She was a sweet, nice girl. National Honor Society. Played field hockey. Organized a Students Against Drunk Driving club at the high school. Never a problem. Her mother and I split when she was about twelve, and she handled it. Loved us both, never acted out. Not like a lot of kids. When I got remarried, she and my new wife hit it off fine. Anyway, the summer after she graduated, I lost her. She was all set to go to college. Westfield State. She planned to be a PE major, wanted to coach and teach. And then she was gone. I mean, she disappeared. Her mother didn't know where she was. Me neither. And I'm a cop." Oakley stopped and rubbed the palm of his hand across his forehead. "Look," he said. "I won't drag this out. She turned up in Boston. She was living with this bastard—this guy. She was hooking for him, getting money for him so he could buy drugs for the two of them. He was an older guy, a Vietnam vet, a burnt-out crazy bastard who carried knives and guns. A Boston cop found her for me, told me where she hung out, a bar in Dorchester, for Chrissake, and she was living with this guy, and I went there ready to kill the son of a bitch, and I was gonna bring Janie home. Something happened. I don't know. They were gone. Disappeared." He shrugged. "That was seven years ago. I don't know where she is. I still don't know."

Oakley looked up. Cammie had been staring at him while he talked. He gave her a quick smile. "I know this isn't your problem, Miss," he said. "And maybe I made it your problem, and if I did I am really sorry. See, she was . . . I can't tell you about the big empty place that's always there inside of me, and how loving my little girl is a lot like hating her for what she did to herself. I hated that guy, that was easy. But I hated her, too. It's as if she was two people, one of them my beautiful little girl and the other one somebody different who ruined her. She did it to herself. I blamed her for that." He shook his head. "This probably doesn't make any sense. See, when you showed up with McCloud, and then I found out about you, what you'd been into, it was like you were the bad half of my Janie, and he was that bastard who ruined her, and . . ."

He looked at Chief Padula, who stared back at him without expression. Oakley shook his head. "Fuck it," he mumbled. "I'm sorry, that's all. I just couldn't stand it, seeing you with him and his drugs and knowing that he had ruined you just the same way that other screwed-up Vietnam vet had ruined my girl. I wanted to save you. I tried to keep an eye on you, to protect you. Maybe it didn't look that way. When I arrested him, that was a good bust. It wasn't just me. But in my head I was doing it for you. To get him away from you. For your own good."

He stared down at the tabletop for a moment. Then he blew out a loud breath and glanced up. His eyes moved from Cammie to me to Padula, then returned to Cammie. "Look," he said quietly. "I got nothing against vets. I did a tour in country myself. But it works two ways, you know? I mean, it messed up a lot of guys. I don't really blame them. But a lot of them never got better. I just figured McCloud was one of them. Like the guy Janie . . ."

He shrugged.

"I wanted to put him away somewhere where he couldn't ruin you anymore. I guess cops aren't supposed to think that way. But I did. I admit it. Anyway, something happened. He got off. I blamed you for that, Mr. Coyne." He glanced at me. "If it wasn't for you, McCloud would've gone to prison and she would've been okay." He turned to Cammie. "And I hated you, God help me. But I loved you, too, and I wanted to protect you. Does this make any sense to you?"

"No," whispered Cammie.

"You had it wrong," I said. "Daniel McCloud saved Cammie. He wasn't the one who ruined her. He rescued her from it."

Oakley stared hard at me. "I don't buy that shit," he

said softly. He took a deep breath and let it out slowly. "The cops all knew what she'd been into," he said. "And I knew what he was after. McCloud, I mean. I could see. I knew. He was old enough to be her father, and he grew enough dope in that garden to keep the whole town stoned. There were times when I wanted to kill them both. And sometimes I just wanted to grab her and take her away. What I mainly did, though, was I watched over her. I figured I could protect her. I was just . . . I kept seeing Janie . . ."

Oakley slumped back in his chair, shaking his head. "I'm sorry," he mumbled. "That's all. I'm just sorry."

I looked at Chief Francis Padula. "You knew all this?"

He shrugged. "He didn't do any harm. He followed the book. I understood. I thought he was right. About Miss Russell and McCloud, I mean."

"He was wrong," said Cammie. "It was Daniel who kept me going."

"Well, it's a good thing Sergeant Oakley was here tonight," said Padula quietly.

26

It was after one in the morning when Oakley and Chief Padula finally left. Cammie and I poured the dregs from the coffeepot into our mugs and topped it off with Wild Turkey. We went into the living room. Cammie put on one of Daniel's Jimmy Reed tapes. We sat close together on the sofa and sipped and hummed.

Once she said, "Thinking of him?"

"Daniel?"

"Yes."

"I was, as a matter of fact."

"I don't understand much of it," she said.

I shrugged. "Me neither, really."

After a while Cammie squirmed against me and rested her cheek on my chest. My arm went around her shoulders. We dozed until the tape ended.

Cammie yawned and stood up. "Ready for bed?"

"Yeah," I said. "Time to hit the road."

"That's really dumb. We've got to give our depositions

at nine in the morning. By the time you get home, you'll have to turn around and come back."

"Good point," I said. "I'll take the sofa."

"You don't have to sleep on the sofa, Brady."

"The sofa will be fine."

She looked at me for a moment, then smiled. "Okay. I'll get some blankets for you."

We were sipping coffee in the kitchen. The early-morning sun was streaming through the windows. When the phone rang, Cammie picked it up.

She said, "Hello?" and then listened for two or three minutes without saying anything. Then she said, "He's here. I'll tell him," and hung up.

She turned to me. "That was Chief Padula. He says they don't need our depositions."

"That's impossible."

She shrugged. "It's what he said."

"Did he say why?"

"Nope."

"Will he want them sometime later, is that it?"

"That's not what he said. He said they wouldn't be needing them, everything was under control, and thanks for all the help."

"You sure you understood properly?"

"Dammit, Brady," said Cammie softly.

I went over to her and hugged her. "I'm sorry," I said. I kissed her hair. "It makes sense, I guess. They got Daniel's case dismissed. Then they quashed the investigation of his murder. This fits. Are you going to be all right?"

I felt her nod against my chest.

"I better go, then," I said.

"I know."

"Let's keep in touch."

"Right," she said. "Give me a call sometime."

"I will," I said.

"Or just drop in. Anytime. I'll be here."

"Sure."

She tilted up her face. I kissed her forehead, found my briefcase, and headed back to the city.

At seven-fifteen Thursday morning Charlie called me. "You awake?" he said.

"Still on my first caffeine injection. Go slow with me."

"Nine o'clock. My office."

"I can't."

"You've got to."

"Is this . . . ?"

"You gotta be there, Brady."

It was the tone of his voice, not his words, that convinced me. "Okay. I may be a few minutes late."

"Brady, hang on a minute," said Charlie. "Man here wants to speak to you."

I waited, then a soft, cultured voice said, "Mr. Coyne?"

"Yes."

"My name is Philip Varney. I'm delighted that we'll be meeting."

I said nothing.

"You, um, you have in your possession, I believe, some government property that we'd like returned."

"Six photographs."

"Exactly. Thank you. I look forward to seeing you."

Philip Varney. PV. From Al Coleman's notes.

I got to my office a few minutes after eight-thirty. Julie wouldn't be in for another half hour. I loaded up the coffee machine and left a note on her desk. "Unscheduled meeting. Should be back by ten. Kisses, BLC."

I went into my sanctum and emptied the contents of my briefcase onto my desk. The envelope with the photographs and index cards. The printout Charlie had given me. Al Coleman's photocopied notes. My .38. I put all of it into my office safe. Then I gathered up the assorted manila folders, loose papers, and fly-fishing catalogs from my desktop and stuffed my briefcase full.

I took the briefcase out to the reception area and sat at Julie's desk to wait for the coffee machine to finish its job. When it did I poured myself a mugful and sipped it with a Winston.

It was five minutes of nine when I picked up my brief-case, locked up, and headed over to Government Center. It would be a twenty-minute walk.

"This is Phil Varney," said Charlie when Shirley ushered me into his office.

He was a gangly guy with dark-rimmed glasses and sparse graying hair brushed straight back from his high shiny forehead. His jacket hung over a chair and his necktie was pulled loose and his cuffs were rolled up past his bony wrists. He looked as if he'd been at work for a long time already this morning. He was leaning against the wall tapping the bowl of a cold pipe in the palm of his hand. He came to me with his hand extended. "Pleasure, Mr. Coyne," he said.

I shook his hand and nodded.

"Have a seat," he said.

"I'll stand," I said. "I've only got a minute."

"Let's all sit," said Charlie.

I shrugged and sat down. Charlie and Varney sat, too.

"FBI?" I said to Varney. "CIA? DEA? What?"

He glanced at Charlie, who said, "Don't ask, Brady. Just listen. Okay?"

"Sure. Okay."

Varney cleared his throat. "You did bring our property with you?"

I patted my briefcase.

He smiled. "Well, good. Why don't you just give it to me and we can all get back to work."

"Sure," I said. "I've just got a couple of questions first."

"Brady . . ." began Charlie.

"I know," I said. "What I don't know won't hurt me." I looked at Varney. "Okay? Can I ask you a couple of things?"

He stopped tapping his palm with his empty pipe and pointed the stem at me. "Charlie's right," he said quietly.

I propped my briefcase up on my lap. "It's only fair."

Varney shrugged. I would have sworn he was going to

say, "It's your funeral." What he actually said was "What do you want to know?"

Varney began to stuff the bowl of his pipe from a leather pouch. I lit a Winston. "I know that Daniel McCloud killed eight people," I said. "I know two of them were small-time criminals, and I know his motive for those was personal. I also know that Brian Sweeney, Daniel's best friend, killed him and Al Coleman. My first question, Mr. Varney. Daniel was killed because he'd written a book about the eight killings, and Coleman was killed because he'd read the book and he wouldn't give it to you. Right?"

Varney took his time firing up his pipe. In a moment Charlie's office was filled with pipe smoke. It was the kind of smoke that reminded me of summer campfires beside a trout river and October bonfires, a good rich masculine smoke.

Those perfumed tobaccos make me gag.

Varney gazed at me through the smoke. "Right," he said.

"And you sent Sweeney after me because I had the photographs."

He nodded. "Not to kill you, Mr. Coyne. You didn't know enough to warrant killing. Just to get our property back."

"He broke into my place. Didn't find it. Shoved an arrow into my bed."

"Sweeney had an unfortunate flair for the dramatic sometimes. But he was very good."

"He was going to kill me, and Cammie Russell, too."

Varney shrugged. "Our people are highly trained. They're expected to use their judgment."

"Improvise," I said. "Do whatever's necessary."

"We try to avoid killing whenever possible," said Varney.

"Incriminating, those photographs. Assignments. Daniel's assignments. He was supposed to destroy those photos, wasn't he?"

Varney turned to Charlie. Charlie said, "Brady, shit. Leave it, will you?"

"I can't," I said.

Varney stared at me for a moment. Then he said, "You're right, Mr. Coyne. Daniel McCloud assassinated those six men. He did it well, and he was well paid for it. We assumed he had destroyed the photographs per his instructions."

"A highly trained Special Forces soldier with skills adaptable to the home front," I said.

Varney puffed his pipe and nodded.

"Wet work."

Varney glanced at Charlie, then turned and smiled at me. "If you wish," he said.

"Why'd he do it?" I said.

"Well, of course, the local police quickly identified him as the prime suspect in the William Johnson killing. It was sloppy. Performed with more passion than finesse. So, in a nutshell, we made a deal with him."

"You got him off the hook for Boomer. In return, he was to provide services for you."

Varney spread his hands. "Yes. Exactly. Now you know."

"You paid him well."

"Handsomely."

"You got the marijuana charges dismissed."

"It was the least we could do."

"He killed Carmine Repucci, too."

"That was his, not ours. We let him have it. Sort of a bonus."

"And later you sent Sweeney to kill him."

"Mr. Coyne," said Varney, "I trust I don't even need to remind you that if a single word of this conversation should ever be heard outside these office doors—"

"You'd deny it," I said. "I know how the government works, and you're right. You don't need to remind me. Pretty damn effective, denial. And without the photographs or Daniel's manuscript, who'd believe such a wild story? It would be stupid and fruitless for me to say anything about this."

He smiled and nodded. "We understand each other, then."

"Good," I said. "Tell me about Sweeney."

"Not much to tell. McCloud had suggested him to us, and we approached him. He was more than willing. Very proficient in his own right, Sweeney. Did some very good work for us. And then he was the obvious candidate for the McCloud job."

"And the Al Coleman job, too."

"Yes, Mr. Coyne. And the Coleman job, too."

"Because he knew too much. Right?"

Varney's pipe had gone out. He puffed at it without effect. He frowned at it, then laid it on Charlie's desk. "I think that's enough, Mr. Coyne."

"One more thing," I said.

He shook his head. "Enough, okay?"

"Who were those six men?" I persisted. "The men in the photographs."

Varney sighed."You could probably guess."

I shrugged. "Government enemies. Men beyond the reach of the courts. Like that?"

"That's it, Mr. Coyne," he said. "End of discussion."

"Yeah, okay," I nodded. "I do have one more question." I turned to Charlie, who had been sitting there quietly staring out of his window. "Charlie," I said.

He turned to look at me.

"You knew all this?"

"Me?" He smiled. "Shit, no. Oh, I suspected something other than an electronic snafu when I lost those names off the computer. That's why I tried so hard to ram it through your concrete skull that you should back off. Otherwise?" He shrugged.

I turned to Varney and lifted my eyebrows. He nodded. "Charlie knew nothing of this."

"Then why are we here?"

"Here? You mean in this office?"

"Yes."

"Would you have met me anywhere else, Mr. Coyne?" said Varney.

"Probably not."

"I worry about you," said Charlie.

"I know," I said. "I'm glad."

"Well, then," said Varney. "Those photographs?"

"Sure," I said. I unsnapped my briefcase and dug into it. I rummaged around, then looked up at him. "Damn," I said.

"What?" said Varney.

"I thought they were here." I dumped out my brief-case onto Charlie's desk and pretended to look through all the papers. Then I snapped my fingers. "I remember now," I said.

"God damn it, Coyne," said Varney.

I shrugged. "Sorry. I'll have to get them for you."

"Damn right you will. Let's go."

"No. Not now. I've got to be in court today. Meet me at Locke-Ober's at five-thirty. I'll have the photos with me."

"You better—"

I held up my hand. "Anyone who can arrange the murders of ten men doesn't need to threaten me. I'll be at Locke's bar at five-thirty, Mr. Varney."

He looked at me for a moment; then he smiled. "That'll be fine, Mr. Coyne." He held out his hand.

I shook it. "I'll see you then."

Charlie walked me out of his office, leaving Varney behind. "I hope the hell you know what you're doing," he whispered to me.

"Hey," I said. "I forgot the photographs."

He squeezed my arm. Hard. "Sure you did."

27

I got back to my office around ten-thirty. Julie looked up at me. "You said ten," she said.

"You know me."

She smiled in spite of herself. "Coffee?"

"I'll get it." I went to the machine and poured two mugs full. I gave one to Julie, then took the chair across from her desk. I lit a cigarette. "What've we got today?"

"It's all on your desk, Brady. I had to rearrange some things. You're pretty packed in from eleven on."

"Cancel everything."

"Oh, no, you don't. You can't—"

"Julie," I said, "I'll make it up to you. But you've got to do your thing. Tell them whatever you've got to tell them. Reschedule everything."

She frowned at me. "This isn't fishing, is it?"

"No."

"Something more important."

"Than fishing?" I pretended to dwell on that question. "I'm not sure I'd go that far. But it's pretty damn important."

I reached The Honorable Chester Y. Popowski in his chambers at the East Cambridge courthouse at five of eleven. Pops always takes a recess at quarter of eleven—out of deference to his aging prostate, he says—and his secretaries all know me well enough to put me through to him.

Pops sits on the Superior Court bench. He's been there for several years. We were classmates and friends at Yale. Now he's one of my clients. "Hey, Brady," he said into the phone.

"You finish taking your leak?"

"Blessedly, yes. What's up?"

"What time do you expect to go into recess this afternoon?"

"Oh, the usual. Four, four-fifteen, at the latest. Wanna buy me a drink?"

"I do want to do that. And I will, as payment for the favor you're going to do for me. But not today."

"What's today?"

"I just want your signature."

"Sounds mysterious."

"It is. And it will remain so. I'll be there at four-fifteen."

"I'll be here."

• • •

"Call Zerk for me," I said to Julie. "If he's not in, have him get back to me. Make sure it's understood that this is very important."

She snapped me a quick salute. "Aye, aye, sir."

Julie knows when not to ask questions.

I spent the next two hours at my typewriter, getting it all down.

My phone rang a couple of minutes after one.

"I've got Zerk for you," said Julie.

"Good," I said. I pressed the blinking button on the console. "Zerk, I need a favor," I said.

Several years earlier, when Julie was out on maternity leave, Xerxes Garrett clerked for me in return for my tutelage on his law boards. He passed and set up a practice in North Cambridge that has evolved into the mirror image of my practice. My clients tend to be wealthy, and therefore elderly and white. Zerk's are mostly poor, young, and black.

He's the best criminal defense lawyer I know. If he wanted to, he could become very rich very fast. So far he's resisted it, for which I admire him enormously.

He's also one of my trusted friends, for which I am grateful.

"Darlene say you been phoning me, man," he said. "Something about urgent."

"More like important," I said. "You in court this afternoon?"

"That's where I'm at right now. Another three minutes and I go try to keep Ellen Whiting's boy Artie out of prison. He not a bad boy, she says."

"You're at East Cambridge?"

"I practically live here."

"Meet me in Judge Popowski's chambers at four-fifteen, can you?"

"I'll be there."

"Bring your notary seal with you."

"Heavy paperwork, huh?"

"Yes. Heavy paperwork."

Julie went out for sandwiches. I chose that time to use the photocopier. I didn't want to risk her seeing a thing. By the time she came back with our tuna on onion rolls, I had the two manila envelopes stashed in my briefcase.

Pops and Zerk were both there when I arrived. They were munching carrot sticks from a plastic bag on top of Pops's desk. When I went in and took the chair beside Zerk, Pops shoved the bag at me. I held up my hand and lit a cigarette instead.

"This'll only take a minute," I said.

"And you're not going to tell us what it's all about," said Pops.

"Right. You don't want to know." I rummaged in my briefcase and removed the envelope that contained the originals.

I had typed three single-spaced pages. At the bottom of each I had left two lines. One for my signature and one for a witness. I spread the three sheets of dense typing on Pops's desk. "I'm now going to affix my signature to each of these pages," I said to the two of them. "After each one, Pops will sign to attest. Then Zerk will notarize our signatures."

My two friends both nodded.

"You won't read these pages," I said.

"We ain't so dumb," said Zerk.

I nodded. "A fountain pen would give it the right flair," I said to Pops.

He handed me the one he always wears in his shirt pocket.

I wrote my signature on the bottom of each page. Pops signed as witness. Zerk squeezed his notary public seal beside the signatures. Then I put the three sheets of paper back into the big envelope, along with the smaller envelope that held the six photographs and two index cards, the computer printouts from Charlie, and the two photocopies from Al Coleman's notebooks.

"Tape," I said to Pops.

He rummaged in the drawer of his desk and handed me a roll of cellophane tape. I taped up the envelope.

"Pen again," I said.

Pops handed his pen to me.

I wrote across the envelope: "In the event of my demise, convey all contents unopened to Mickey Gillis at the *Boston Globe*." I signed my name under it.

I handed the envelope to Zerk. He looked at it, then looked up at me. He showed it to Pops.

"Demise," said Zerk, grinning. "Shee-it!"

"A technical term," I said.

"Mickey Gillis," he said. "That reporter who's got the hots for you."

"That one," I said. "Not exactly hots. More like luke-warms."

"This for when you get offed."

"This for *if* I get offed."

"You want me to keep it for you, man?"

"Keep it secure, Zerk. Tell no one you've got it. Tell no one you met with me today. You, either," I said to Pops.

They both shrugged.

"Well, thanks." I stood up. "Drinks for both of you. Next week sometime." I shook hands with each of them and turned to leave.

"Wait," said Zerk. "I'll go down with you."

"No. I'll go down alone."

Zerk turned to Pops. "Heavy paperwork," he said, weighing the envelope in his two hands and nodding solemnly.

Phil Varney was perched on a barstool just inside the entrance to Locke's. I climbed onto the empty one beside him and placed my briefcase on the bar. Varney glanced at it, then at his watch. "You're right on time, Mr. Coyne," he said.

"I wouldn't have missed it," I said. I caught the bartender's eye. "Daniel's, rocks," I told him.

We didn't say anything until my drink was delivered. Then Varney held his glass at me. "To the satisfactory completion of our business," he said.

I clicked his glass and sipped my drink.

"Well," he said, "let's have it, then."

I removed the manila envelope from my briefcase and handed it to him. He opened it and removed all the papers. He glanced through them, frowned up at me, shuffled through the papers again. Then he carefully put his glass down on the bar and said softly, "What the fuck is this, Coyne?"

"Pretty self-evident, isn't it?"

"Photocopies? All photocopies? And this . . . this fucking document?" He waved the copies of the three pages I had typed and signed and Pops had witnessed and Zerk had notarized. The copies, of course, had no signatures on them. "What the Christ is this?"

"You can read it at your leisure," I said. "I think I got it all down. Not, of course, in the same detail as Daniel McCloud's manuscript. But enough, I think. I signed the originals, and my signatures have been witnessed and notarized. The photographs—you see I've photocopied them for you, just to verify for you that I have them—they're with the document, as is an assortment of corroborating stuff, copies of which you have there. The originals of everything are in a safe place, where they will remain."

I took another sip of my drink, then lit a cigarette.

"Unless something happens to you," said Varney in a low voice.

"Oh, right," I said. "In that case, the newspapers get everything."

"You're playing a dangerous game, Coyne."

"The way I see it, this is less dangerous than all the alternatives I could think of. Look at it this way. It protects both of us. It's in your interest to make sure nothing happens to me. And it's in my interest to make sure nobody hears a word about any of this." I tapped my fingers on the papers on the bar. "Tit for tat. Good deal all around, huh?"

Varney stared at me for a long moment. Then he smiled. "I guess we understand each other."

"I hope so."

"We're not that different, you and I," he said.

"I'm not flattered."

He shrugged and smiled again. "We think the same way." He gathered up the papers and slid them into the envelope. "One thing still puzzles me," he said.

"What's that?"

"Sweeney couldn't come up with any copies of McCloud's book."

"Not for lack of trying," I said, remembering how the little office in back of Daniel's shop had been tossed.

"Now that we've got this—this stalemate between us, I was wondering . . ."

"I don't think there is a copy," I said. "Sweeney got the original for you. There's nothing among Daniel's things. I don't have one. Al Coleman's wife doesn't have one."

"Let us both hope nobody has one," he said.

"Which reminds me," I said. "If anything should happen to Cammie Russell or Bonnie Coleman, the deal changes."

"And if a copy of that manuscript turns up in the wrong hands, Mr. Coyne, the deal's emphatically off."

"I think we both understand the deal, then," I said.

He nodded. "We do. And it's a good deal all around. You want another drink?"

"I wouldn't mind."

28

On the last Sunday in January I drove out to Wilson Falls. Cammie and I held hands and walked along the shoreline of the Connecticut. The muddy banks were frozen solid. The bays and edges of the river were iced over, but out in the middle open water marked the main channel.

Snow had fallen, melted, and fallen again through the halting progression of the New England winter. The landscape was all white, daubed here and there in ocher, sepia, burnt sienna. Tree skeletons poked up through the snow, stark black, and splashes of dark green marked groves of evergreens. Chickadees and nuthatches flitted among the leafless bushes.

It was one of those transparent winter days when the sun shines so bright and ricochets so hard off the ice and water and snow that it seems to slice through the air, and even wearing sunglasses I had to squint the pain out of my eyes. The sun carried no warmth. Just light. Cammie and I wore ski parkas and wool hats and gloves. We walked slowly, picking our way over the logjams and boulders along the rim of the river. Cammie talked about Daniel. She missed him, but she was healing. She didn't ask me any difficult questions, for which I was grateful. It saved me the trouble of lying to her.

I pointed out the place where Daniel first took me fishing. It seemed like a very long time ago. A little farther along, we stopped for a moment at the spot where Sergeant Richard Oakley shot Brian Sweeney.

Both places looked different under the ice.

We walked until the shadows grew long and the sun began to settle behind the low hills across the river. Then we turned back.

Cammie made hot chocolate. We played our favorite Jimmy Reed tape. Outside, darkness fell fast. We sat in rocking chairs by the woodstove, sipping our cocoa and staring at our stockinged feet.

"Have you talked with Terri?" said Cammie.

"Not for a long time. I think as soon as we decide we can be friends without being lovers, we will talk."

"It's good to be friends."

"Yes."

"Better, sometimes."

"Yes." I reached my hand to her.

She grasped it and squeezed it and held on. We continued to study our feet. "I've decided to leave, Brady."

I sipped my cocoa and said nothing.

"Vinnie and Roscoe are taking over Daniel's shop. With Brian gone, it's theirs free and clear. They want to buy all this from me." She waved her free hand around. "We're working out the details."

"What will you do?"

She gave my hand a squeeze and then let go. "I'm going home," she said. "I've got some money now. I'll buy my mother a proper house, build myself a little studio. I want to paint the mountains. In the mornings, with that wonderful early light, there's a mist that comes off them. I think I can capture that."

"It sounds good, Cammie."

"Now, without Daniel, that's where I should be. It's where I belong."

I found myself nodding. I turned to look at Cammie. She was smiling softly at me, and I could see the question in her eyes.

Where do *you* belong? they were asking.

But Cammie did not ask me that question.

I was glad she didn't, because I couldn't have answered it.

ABOUT THE AUTHOR

WILLIAM G. TAPPLY is the author of eleven previous Brady Coyne mysteries. A contributing editor to *Field & Stream*, he has published several collections of essays on hunting and fishing. His most recent book is a memoir of his father called *Sportsman's Legacy*. Tapply lives in Acton, Massachusetts.